the frog, the wizard, and the shrew

Mary Ann Myers

LIGHTHOUSE
Literary Press, Inc.
Chesterland, Ohio

Lighthouse Literary Press, Inc.
P.O. Box 421
Chesterland, Ohio 44026

First Edition
10 9 8 7 6 5 4 3 2 1

This is a work of fiction. Names, characters, places, and incidents
either are the products of the author's imagination or are used
fictitiously, and any resemblance to actual persons, living or dead,
events, or locales is entirely coincidental.

Publisher's Cataloging-in-Publication
(Provided by Quality Books, Inc.)

Myers, MaryAnn, 1950-

    The frog, the wizard, and the shrew / MaryAnn Myers.
-- Ist ed.
    P. cm.
    LCCN 00-192156
    ISBN 0-9668780-3-5

    1. Fantastic fiction. 1. Title.

PS3563.Y442F76 2001   813'.54

                QBIOO-901551

The Frog, the Wizard, and the Shrew
is dedicated to the Cook Forest Gang.
Hedy, Jean, Judy and Pat.
May it never end.

My Grandmother Light sensed things. Not happy things. Weird things, sad things. One day for instance, she dropped a dish in the sink, stared hard out the window and said right out of the blue, "Get me to the mine, there's been a cave-in." The mine was six miles away, too far to walk or to hear, and too far to feel the earth move. But sure enough, my Grandfather John was trapped. He survived to go down into the shaft again and again, but that day my grandmother paced back and forth knowing. "He can't breathe," she kept saying. "He can't breathe and he hasn't eaten lunch. I made him pork and I can smell it." Years later he died hungry, but I'm told from that day my grandmother treated him different. "I miss him already," she would say, and him sitting right there beside her. I was named after my grandmother and was supposed to have inherited her sense of things. "Open your eyes and listen," she would say. And I knew what she meant. Still, all things considered, when the past came to haunt me, I can honestly say I never saw it coming.

Anne Marie

CHAPTER ONE

Anne Marie climbed the last flight of stairs to her apartment on the fourth floor, trudged all the way down the hall, unlocked the door, and crumpled into a heap, devastated. She stared at her private world. The overstuffed couch, the oriental rug, the CD player with surround-sound speakers, (ninety days same as cash) her bean-bag chair and the no-smoking sign; all that was left of Jimmie, her bed, (Victorian) he called it, and the cactus.

By most standards, it wasn't much. But it was everything she had. And she liked it here. It was home.

Why me, she thought, and read the eviction notice over and over. She had a week.

"I don't think they can do that," Judy said later, when visiting. "I think you should get a lawyer."

It had taken Anne Marie so very long to find this place.

"What did they give for the reason?"

"They're tearing the building down and putting up a strip mall."

"You're kidding."

"No." Anne Marie shook her head. She'd never kid about something like that.

"So what are you going to do?"

"Move. What else?"

Judy sighed. She could suggest Anne Marie stay with her and Phil for a while in the event she didn't find anything right away. But the two of them would be at each other's throats in a day. "The man hunts down animals for fun," she could hear Anne Marie saying at the sight of his camouflage. "Who does he pick on when he's in a bad mood?" Which in Anne Marie's opinion was all the time.

"What about your mom?"

Anne Marie looked at her.

"Sorry."

Anne Marie's mom was the last person she'd turn to. "Let's go down to Vince's and get a paper." Vince's was the corner drug store. That's the kind of neighborhood this was, moms and pops, no trouble, and only one felon. Phil. Until lately.

Anne Marie grabbed her purse, winced and said something about her shoulder being sore, and off they went.

"What did you do to it?"

"I don't know," she said. "But it's been hurting for about a week. I must have strained something."

Six days later, practically down to the wire, Anne Marie found another apartment and moved. Phil, to his credit, helped, but damaged the cactus, and Judy hustled him out fast. "Call me when you get your phone in," she yelled from the car window.

Anne Marie nodded, debating what to do. If she were back home at her old place, she could ask Mr. Murphy's advice. A cactus is a delicate thing. She sat down on the worn linoleum floor and stared in agony. When she'd bought it, it wasn't but a foot high, and had grown over the years to stand as tall as she. It was bent at the waist now. She carefully lifted the end, surveyed the damage and brought it back down gently. How could it live like this? Traumatized.

A knock on the door startled her, enough so that for a second all she did was sit there, frozen in time, so to speak. "Who is it?" she finally said.

"Your neighbor," a thready, elderly-sounding female voice responded. "Miss Colorado."

"Miss Colorado?" Anne Marie frowned, gave the cactus another helpless glance, and got up and opened the door.

"Hello, there," a little woman standing no more than four-foot or considerably less said. "Welcome." She extended her tiny hand, all smiles, and introduced herself again, "Miss Colorado, Daisy Colorado."

"Hi," Anne Marie said, trying to mask her amusement. "It's nice to meet you. I'm Anne Marie. Anne Marie Light."

"Wonderful. What a lovely name. I'm from across the hall, I used to be in the circus."

Anne Marie smiled. She could picture her there.

"Is this your first apartment alone?" Miss Colorado asked, donning thick glasses and looking Anne Marie up and down.

Anne Marie shook her head. The woman's eyes were now magnified ten times over. "My second."

"How old are you?"

"Twenty-six," Anne Marie said.

Miss Colorado peered closer into Anne Marie's face, nodded, and took off her glasses and turned to leave. "Well, like I said, welcome. I'm right across the hall."

Anne Marie watched as the little woman made her way back, watched how she felt for her door and then the handle, and marveled as she disappeared.

"Hey there," a casual voice to her right said.

She leaned out.

It was a middle-aged man, checking his mailbox.

"How's it going?" he asked, glancing at her.

"Okay," she said. "How about you?"

He shrugged, and with that, disappeared behind the next door. Anne Marie retreated as well and spent the next few hours unpacking. This apartment was basically smaller than her other one, but had a separate bedroom and a bathroom with an old clawfoot tub. The tub in her opinion was a major drawback. She was a shower person. Showers were quick and to the point. Eventually she found herself back on the floor in front of the cactus, wondering what to do, and knew sooner or later, that whatever it was, it was going to hurt.

CHAPTER TWO

Anne Marie walked out of the doctor's office in a fog. "Go," her co-workers had said. "Find out what's wrong." So she went, and didn't know any more now than she did before.

"A possible strain."

"But it started in my shoulder and now it hurts in my elbow. No, I don't play tennis. No, I didn't fall." Lift anything heavy? She shook her head. No heavier than usual. "No."

"Here's a prescription for a muscle relaxant. Take them twice a day."

I'd rather not, Anne Marie thought, and tossed it in the trash as she exited the elevator. But then, "Oh no," she said, hurrying back to retrieve it when the thought of someone else filling it crossed her mind. She ripped it into pieces.

"Are you sure it's not my heart?" she'd asked. After all, Jimmie did do a number on it.

"No, your heart is fine. You're fine. You just need to relax. You worry too much."

Okay. Anne Marie jogged across the street, darted in front of a bus, raised her arm to hail the driver, and gasped as a sharp pain shot through her elbow. I wouldn't worry if it didn't hurt, she told herself, thanking the driver even as he swore at her with his eyes.

"Sorry. I was in a hurry," she told him.

"What, to die?" he asked.

She shook her head and took a seat. The telephone company was due at her apartment in twenty minutes. When she made the appointment, she hadn't expected to wait over an hour and a half to see the doctor.

Miss Colorado greeted her from her door without her glasses. "You missed him," she said.

Anne Marie frowned. "Who? The telephone man?" She darted her eyes to Miss Colorado's big clock-face wristwatch. He wasn't due for another five minutes. "Tell me he didn't leave."

"Okay."

Anne Marie sighed a sigh of relief.

"But he did."

"What?"

"He said to tell you you'll have to call and schedule another appointment."

"That creep," Anne Marie said. "He can't do this. I need that phone."

"He was upset with you."

"What? Upset with me? He's the one that was early."

"He said you were inconsiderate."

Anne Marie stared. "Thank you. Thank you for passing that on."

Miss Colorado nodded and closed her door.

Anne Marie entered her apartment and, first thing, looked at the cactus. Her makeshift splint still held it in place, but the tip was browning. She'd planned to call a nursery or florist as soon as the serviceman left. "Sorry," she told it as she tossed her purse on the couch to its side. "I'll call from work tomorrow. Hang in there."

She made a box of vanilla pudding for dinner, ate two bowls of it warm and slightly burnt, and sat herself down in the tub when it was about half full. She felt stupid sitting there, as if she were being watched, washed quickly, and got out and towel dried. It was then, someone pounded on her door.

"Telephone," she heard a voice say.

"Oh wonderful." She yelled she'd be right there, hurried into the bedroom, and pulled on a pair of jeans and a sweater. "I'm coming!"

She opened the door and raised her eyes.

"Since I was still in the neighborhood," the man said.

Anne Marie stepped back for him to enter, a tall man with sandy-blonde hair, nice looking in a way, and with a tattoo on his arm.

"Did you say there's no jacks anywhere?" he said, glancing around as if that were a ridiculous notion.

"Yes, that's why I called. I looked everywhere."

"Well, according to the records, there's one here somewhere," he said, and started searching. The kitchenette was small, no jack there.

He checked the three walls in the living room, the four walls in the bedroom. She was glad she'd made the bed. Then he headed into the bathroom.

"I hardly doubt..." she started to say, following him.

"Well, look at here."

There it was, behind the toilet. He gazed at her in a somewhat critical fashion. "I thought you said you looked."

She sighed. Who'd think to look there? She noticed the tub then, her bath water still in it, and hugged her arms to her sides. She'd have to learn to pull the plug before getting out. "How long is this going to take?" she asked, and it was then, as he stepped back, that she noticed her underwear on the floor at his feet. He held up his hands, a gesture she took to mean he'd already noticed them, and she reached down to pick them up out of the way.

"Sorry," she mumbled, blushing. And he smiled.

She walked out then, and went in and sat on her bed, underwear still in hand, and stared at the wall.

"Anne Marie," he said.

She turned, half expecting to see a ghost of someone she knew standing in the doorway, he'd said her name so.... "Yes?"

"I'm going down to my truck. I'll be right back."

She nodded, as if he could see her from the front door, and tucked her underwear beneath the blanket. "Okay."

She ran a brush through her hair, put on her slippers to go into the kitchen, busied herself with doing up the few dishes and one pan in the sink, and decided to scour the pan again after he returned.

He hummed as he worked, doing whatever it was he was doing. If the jack was there, she couldn't imagine what was taking him so long. She looked around the kitchen for something to do. Nothing. She'd already scrubbed it from top to bottom.

"All done," he said, and she jumped.

"Thank you," she managed.

He nodded, and started writing her up a service bill.

"How much is this going to cost?" she asked, glancing at the tattoo on his arm.

He shrugged. "That's not my department. You should've asked the office."

Anne Marie looked at him. "Actually I did. But that was when I didn't think I had a jack. I assume that'll have some bearing."

The man smiled, that same smile from in the bathroom.

"And while I'm at it," she said. "I am not inconsiderate. I'm the most considerate person I know."

Another smile. "Well, good for you." He handed her the service bill and tipped his pen toward her bunny slippers. "Cute," he said.

She followed him to the door, and bolted the locks in his wake. The slippers were a present from her mother two Christmases ago. She walked over to the window, looked out, watched as he got in behind the wheel of his truck, and turned, startled when the phone rang.

She stared, motionless, a habit that used to drive Jimmie crazy, and a second later hurried past the cactus and into the bathroom to answer it. "Hello."

"Hello. Just testing," the man said.

Anne Marie smiled, noticing the long cord he'd left her.

"Thank you."

"No problem."

CHAPTER THREE

Though Anne Marie liked her secretarial job at the Headlands Employment Agency, a high-powered company nicknamed Headlands Ink, she'd thought about quitting when Jimmie left her, because it was hard working with him now. After all, he still smelled the same, talked the same and looked the same, and was the same, except for the fact that he was living with another woman. But one change was enough.

"I don't know how you do it," Judy said. "I'd cry every time I saw him if it was Phil."

Anne Marie looked at her. She'd cry too, if it was Phil.

"So, are you going to throw the cactus out?"

"No." It looked like hell, splinted and shriveling. "This guy at the nursery says...."

The phone rang.

"I'll get it," Judy said. "I've gotta pee anyway."

Anne Marie went into the kitchen to wash their coffee cups, emptied the coffee maker, and turned when Judy emerged.

"It was the phone company," she reported. "They wanted to know how the phone was working."

Anne Marie stared. "What did you tell them?"

"I told them it's working fine. Is it working fine?"

"I guess so." Anne Marie shrugged and glanced at the clock on the stove. It was seven thirty-five. A little late for their office to be calling, she thought. "Is that all they wanted?"

"I guess." Judy hopped up on the kitchen counter, frowned when Anne Marie gave her a disparaging look, and slid back down. Anne Marie was such a fussbudget. She wouldn't let her drink out of the milk carton either. "So what about the party, are you going to go?"

Anne Marie walked past her into the living room. "I don't know. Everyone else is going with somebody."

"So. What's the difference?"

Anne Marie looked at her, this, the woman who needed company just to go to the dry cleaners. "I'll feel stupid. They'll ask where Jimmie is, and...."

"No one'll ask," Judy said. "Besides, they all know."

"Wonderful."

"Come on," Judy coaxed. "It's going to be so much fun. They actually have an authentic fifties band."

"Which one?"

Judy shrugged. "I don't know. A doo-wop something. Come on."

Anne Marie stared at the cactus while giving it thought. "I hate dressing up."

"You hate everything."

Anne Marie conceded and smiled. "What are you going to wear?"

"I don't know. I thought we'd go to that vintage shop over on Prospect and look. I want to see if they have any old prom dresses."

Anne Marie glanced at her. "What time?"

"I don't know. Six, six-thirty. Do you want to meet me there?" Prospect was only two blocks from where Anne Marie worked.

Anne Marie shrugged.

"Good, I'll see you there."

Anne Marie walked with her out into the hall, a thought crossing her mind then. "When the phone company called, was it a man or a woman?"

"A woman, why?"

"Just wondering."

"I'll see you tomorrow."

Miss Colorado appeared out of nowhere as Anne Marie started back in. "Did you hear the noise last night?"

Anne Marie shook her head, still taken aback whenever she saw the tiny little woman. "What noise?"

Miss Colorado motioned to the apartment next door, rolled her distant eyes, and pressed her hand to her heart. "We should've never gone over there."

"Where?"

"Vietnam. The war."

Anne Marie nodded, understanding now, and glanced at the door to her left. Her neighbor was obviously a veteran.

"Keep your doors locked," Miss Colorado said. "And don't ever let him in when he's like that."

"Like what?"

"You'll know," Miss Colorado said. "You'll know."

Anne Marie told the woman good night and went back inside. The phone rang as she was locking the doors, but quit before she could get to it, and she wondered who it was. It's not as if a lot of people had the number. It rang again and she picked it up.

"Hello."

Silence.

"Hello."

Click.

Anne Marie put the lid down on the toilet and sat staring at the wall. At times in her life, she'd had strange feelings about things, and this was one of them. The person who called hadn't meant to hang up, probably didn't want to hang up, but hung up anyway for some reason. And would phone again. It was just a matter of when.

Anne Marie thought about the man next door, leaned over to put the plug in the tub, and started her bath water. Jimmie used to tell her that when she stared the way she was staring now, she was in another world, one he didn't care to visit. And he'd always laugh, which brought her out of it. She wondered now, with no one to bring her back, if she just might go over to the other side and stay. Maybe it would be nice. Maybe Jimmie wouldn't matter there. Maybe....

The sound of water hitting the linoleum floor eventually crept into her mind, and she groped for the handle. It was like the day with the fire. The grease fire.

"What are you doing?" Jimmie had shouted. "Stand back!" He doused it with flour, all the flour she had, whole wheat flour, and held her hands under cold running water for what seemed like hours.

"I worry about you, Anne," he kept saying. He always called her just Anne. "I really worry about you. I never know what you're going to do next."

"Empty the tub," she told herself. "You're going to empty the tub."

But first, she was going to take a bath, and then mop the floor. And if the phone rang again, she wasn't going to answer it. She drained half the water, stripped and stepped in carefully, and sat down. The warmth felt good on her back, her awkwardness at just sitting there, starting to pass, and she leaned back all the way, the water brimming her shoulders and chin. She remembered being a child, so small and the water so cloudy. "Look, Mommy. The soap floats."

She remembered being scolded. Now was not the time to dawdle. Her mother had things to do, and sitting there while Anne Marie played wasn't one of them. "Hurry up."

Anne Marie reached for the soap, the kind that would sink, and took her time, starting first with her face and neck, down over her breasts and between her legs, and let the phone ring, and ring, and ring.

CHAPTER FOUR

"They're all twenty dollars."

Anne Marie and Judy looked at the sales clerk.

"Next week they'll be ten."

"Why's that?"

"The change of seasons. We put out our fall clothes then."

Judy dragged Anne Marie toward the rack. "Oh my God, look at this!" She seized a powder blue, chiffon formal. "I love it!" This was how Judy shopped. If it fit, she'd be done. Anne Marie on the other hand, took her time and looked and looked. Some had stains. She wondered how each got there.

"What about this one?" Judy held up a pink taffeta.

Anne Marie shook her head. "I'd look like cotton candy."

Judy laughed, took her dress in to try on, and Anne Marie browsed. She checked the size of a black chemise, too small, the navy blue satin and lace, too big, and bored, started humming.

"Oh, I love that song," the clerk said, lighting up.

Anne Marie looked at her. "What?"

"'Blue, Navy Blue.' It's one of my favorite songs."

Anne Marie nodded, though she didn't hear any music herself, and continued on to a rack of pedal pushers, sleeveless blouses, and some one-of-a-kind bathing suits. Again she hummed, and again the clerk seemed entertained.

"Try it on," she said. "It looks like it would fit you."

"What?"

"The 'Itsy Bitsy Teeny Weeny Yellow Polka Dot Bikini.'"

Anne Marie looked at it and smiled. It wasn't exactly a bikini by today's standards, but it was the right color and polka dot. The clerk appeared at her side. "Do you remember that song about big diamond, big blue diamond?" She sang a line. "On your finger...."

Anne Marie shook her head. "I'm sorry. I don't know many songs from that time."

The clerk nodded and sighed. Judy made an entrance from the dressing room then and twirled in front of the mirror. "What do you think?"

"It's pretty," Anne Marie said. "Really pretty."

Judy rolled her eyes and laughed. Anne Marie always sounded so serious, so old fashioned. "I'd rather look hot. Phil's been really tired lately, if you know what I mean."

The clerk chuckled, as if she'd been there. "It's hot. Don't worry."

A half hour later, Anne Marie was still browsing. "Sorry. Do you know of any other shops in the area?"

The woman nodded, perhaps hoping to be rid of them and close early. "There's one on Andrews and Ninth. It's right on the corner."

Anne Marie thanked her, Judy paid for her dress, and the two walked to the next store. But Anne Marie had no luck here either. And on top of that, the place had a smell about it, a musty, sickening mothbally smell. "What?"

"Formaldehyde," Anne Marie said. "I think people were buried in those dresses."

Judy laughed. "So where to now?"

"Nowhere. Go on home." Judy and Phil's "flat", as they liked to call it, was less than five minutes walking distance away. But Anne Marie had to ride the bus back across town and it was going to be dark soon. "I'll find something tomorrow." She motioned to the approaching bus, boarded when it stopped, and waved. "Call me."

Her legs felt like lead as she sat down and settled back, and she wondered why. It's not as if they'd walked that far. She looked out the window at her old building, scheduled for demolition on Monday according to the sign posted out front, and thought about how Jimmie used to yell to her from the street whenever he'd forgotten something. He should have yelled to her the day he forgot....

"Miss."

Anne Marie looked up.

"Your stop," the driver said.

"Oh. Thank you."

Her Vietnam veteran neighbor was sitting on the stoop, drinking a beer. "Hey there." He smiled. "How's it going?"

13

"Okay," she said, noticing how green his eyes were, and how glassy. "How about you?"

He shrugged, end of conversation, and Anne Marie walked on up and inside. For the first time since she'd moved, she was glad for the change. The way her legs were feeling, she couldn't have made it up one full flight, let alone four. She thought about going to the doctor again, but figured he'd only tell her to stop worrying, so she tried to stop worrying. But then her shoulder twinged, and she stretched out on the couch, to worry some more.

"What's wrong with me? I'm falling apart."

She stared at the cactus. "Leave it alone," the man at the nursery had said.

"But what about the splint?"

"Well, you probably shouldn't have done that. Out in the desert...."

"Out in the desert, another cactus might have supported it."

"Still, leave it alone. Water it the same, and see what happens."

She wondered if there was such a thing as a plant doctor, and envisioned one telling her and the cactus not to worry. It's nothing. It's all in your head.

She leaned over the side of the couch, upside down, and looked at the cactus from this perspective and sighed. It was dying, plain as day. Whether from the top or the bottom, didn't matter. It was dying.

"Leave it alone."

"Right." It was all she could do.

Dinner that night would have to be pudding again, since she hadn't gone to the store. At least this batch she didn't burn, and it tasted good warm. Why her mother insisted she wait until it was chilled was beyond her. Be patient.

"Why? I like it like this."

"Too bad. That's not the way it's supposed to be eaten."

Anne Marie helped herself to another bowl.

Jimmie didn't like it warm either.

She thought about her father, father because she never knew him well enough to call him Dad, and wondered how he liked his pudding.

"Who cares?" she could hear her mother say. "The man was a bum."

The man was dead.

Why a fifties dance? I'd blend in better in the sixties, she thought. I could wear something I own. I could tie-dye something. I could pop that pill Jimmie once tried to shove down my throat, and fly. Yes, I could fly.

She heard a thud next door and thought about what Miss Colorado had said. "You'll know." How will I know? Will he be screaming? Crying? Will he pound on the door? Would tonight be the night? Does it start with a beer? Has he had more than one? She looked at the cactus. And stupid as some might think, she thought of how she might protect it if the man were to break the door down and come charging. She couldn't stand the possibilities, and decided to go speak with Miss Colorado. Not a visit exactly, but just to talk to her, to ask her to clarify what she meant.

I won't know. I have no way of knowing.

Miss Colorado opened her door, and looked up.

"Can I talk to you?" Anne Marie asked.

"Sure, dear."

Anne Marie followed her inside and glanced around. The apartment was beautiful. The same size as hers apparently, the same layout, but packed full and furnished like a doll house, everything in its place, everything....

"Wow!"

Miss Colorado smiled and sat herself down in a tiny chair, a munchkin, Anne Marie couldn't help thinking.

"Your apartment is beautiful. How long have you lived here?"

"Oh, about five years."

Anne Marie nodded, then remembered the woman probably couldn't see her since she didn't have her glasses on. "Did you decorate it yourself?"

"Yes." Miss Colorado smiled, a happy smile, a rather contented smile. And yet, at the sight of that smile, tears welled up in Anne Marie's eyes.

"Miss Colorado," she said. "How do you see it?"

"I don't." The little woman hesitated and shrugged. "But that doesn't mean that I don't know that it's there."

Anne Marie tried to swallow the lump forming in her throat. "Is that enough? Just knowing?"

"No. But when you've seen what I've seen, it'll do."
Anne Marie looked at her.
"Would you like some tea, dear?"
Anne Marie nodded. "I'd love some. Thank you."

CHAPTER FIVE

Jimmie called in sick and sounded hung over. He said he'd be in tomorrow. Tomorrow was the dance, and Anne Marie still didn't have a dress. The pink taffeta down the street was looking better and better. She'd stopped twice to make sure it was still there, and now it was in the window.

"Listen," the clerk said. "The sale doesn't start till tomorrow, but for you...."

Anne Marie smiled, figuring she must look poor, and finally tried it on. It was then, as she looked in the mirror and sighed, that she literally stepped back in time. "'Tell Laura I love her.' Tell Laura I didn't leave her. Tell Laura...."

The clerk came up behind her. "It's tell Laura I need her."

"What?"

"The lyrics. It's 'tell Laura I need her.' Not, 'that I didn't leave her.'"

Anne Marie smiled. This woman was so eccentric. But then again. "Tell Laura not to cry. My love for her will never die." She couldn't believe she knew the song. "Are you sure it's not 'tell Laura I didn't leave her'?"

"Positive, honey. You're talking my time. I know them all. That song was sung by Ray Peterson in the summer of 1960. I just wish I knew who sang, 'Big Diamond, Big Blue Diamond.'"

Anne Marie smoothed the dress, at least a size, maybe two, too big, and stared. "How's it go?"

"'Big Diamond, Big Blue Diamond.'"

"On your finger...."

"Right, do you know it?"

Anne Marie shook her head. She just remembered it from the other day. "What time do you open tomorrow?"

"Nine. But I was serious. You can have it for ten today. No one's going to buy it between today and tomorrow."

"Thank you. But I have to come right by here tomorrow anyway. If you'll just hold it for me."

The woman smiled. "What's your last name?"

"Light."

The woman wrote her name on the tag pinned to the dress, hung it in the storeroom, and Anne Marie left and went back to work. She was dreading this afternoon. More cold calls. It was really the agents' job, but when things were slow, and with Jimmie out....

"Hi, my name is Anne Marie Light of the Headlands Employment Agency, and I have an applicant in my office that has a BA in Business and five years' experience." Chances are the company, one she'd just picked randomly out of the phone book, wouldn't have a position for this particular phantom person. But in the course of the conversation, at the odds of about one in ten, the person on the phone might tell her of another opening at that particular company, and voila, the agency's foot was in the door. "A salary range? Just a ballpark figure? And what about benefits? Hours?" It was common practice to comb the classified ads in the paper as well. While most employers running their own ads probably preferred not to go through an employment agency because of the hounding that might ensue, occasionally one who wasn't having any luck independently would decide to list with them.

These calls weren't bad. It was the other nine out of ten that wore thin after a while. Anne Marie missed seeing the dress in the window on the way home, but was superstitious. She didn't want to be treated differently than anyone else. No better and no worse. Besides, even if she were inclined to take the woman up on her offer, tomorrow was payday and she only had nine dollars and seventy-nine cents in her purse, counting the twenty-nine pennies left in the wrapper. And she was proud.

"When you leave here, don't come back asking for my help. You hear me?" her mother had screamed, as Anne Marie packed. "You hear me?!"

Anne Marie heard her, and still heard her. She didn't ask for anything from anybody.

Miss Colorado knocked on her door. "Your telephone man was here."

"What?"

"Your telephone man."

"Why? There's nothing wrong with my phone."

"That's what I said."

Anne Marie smiled. How would she know, she wondered, and reconsidered. She'd know. "What did he say?"

"Nothing. He just said to tell you he was by."

"Well, thank you. Would you like to come in?"

"No." Miss Colorado shook her head, and glanced instinctively toward her door. "I have to get back," she said, as if someone were waiting for her. "Did you find a dress?"

"No, I think I'm just going to go with the pink taffeta. I tried it on."

Miss Colorado smiled. "The cotton candy one?"

"Yes. It's a little big, but...."

"Come show me when you get it. I'll take it in for you. I know cotton candy."

Anne Marie laughed, and watched as she walked to her door, felt for the handle and started into her apartment.

"Miss Colorado?"

"Yes?" The tiny woman peered back and into the distance.

"Do you know anything about cactus?"

"No. Nary a thing. Why?"

"Just wondering. Thanks anyway."

Anne Marie made Spanish Rice-a-Roni for dinner and ate the whole thing, a bowl at a time, standing and staring out the window. Why had the telephone man stopped by? She should've asked what time. If it was before five, then maybe.... She thought about his tattoo. But if it was after five, then....

She stared, heard a siren in the distance, and stared some more. Another siren sounded. Then another. Closer and closer, then further away. A thud against the wall made her jump.

"Shut the fuck up!" she heard her neighbor the vet shout. "I said shut the fuck up!" She heard the sound of broken glass, then another, and another. A whole six pack, she counted. And more thuds and then more shouting. Then crying. Crying like she'd never heard before.

She thought of Miss Colorado, what she'd said about knowing, and knew now, and crouched down on the floor by the cactus. The sirens were gone, long gone, but the man next door was still hearing them, and would for most of the night.

"Don't open your door."

"Don't open your door."

"I won't."

CHAPTER SIX

Anne Marie went to the bank on her lunch hour to cash her paycheck, made a deposit, and headed for the vintage shop. As she passed a Marine Recruiting Office, she thought of her neighbor.

"Incoming, incoming!" he'd shouted again and again. "Get down, get down! Incoming, incoming! Get down, get down!"

She rounded the corner and stopped dead. The sirens last night were for this block. A whole row of businesses. The vintage shop included. She approached slowly, one of many spectators, and stared at the smoldering devastation.

"Oh my God...."

"Sad, isn't it," a man said. "They think it's arson."

"Why?" another said.

"For the insurance."

"Whose?"

Anne Marie shook her head, turned to leave, and noticed the sales clerk standing by the curb, eyes red, and shivering. "A cigarette is what I need," the woman said, when Anne Marie asked if there were anything she could do to help.

"I'm sorry." Anne Marie didn't smoke.

"I don't know what I'm going to do," the woman said with a catch in her throat. "This shop was everything I had."

Anne Marie looked at her, hadn't realized the woman owned the shop and was not only out of a job, but a life. "You're going to start over," Anne Marie said, astonishing even herself with such a bold statement to a virtual stranger.

"How?" the woman said, helplessly. "Even if I had the money, which I don't, I can't go out and buy inventory."

Anne Marie nodded. "You won't have to. That man over there says they suspect arson. And if that's the case...."

The woman looked at her.

"You're going to get donations from everywhere. You'll be surprised."

The woman stared.

"I'll see you," Anne Marie said, and turned to leave.

"Wait."

Anne Marie stopped.

"You're not going to believe this." The woman wiped her eyes. "But you know how I put your dress in back?"

Anne Marie nodded.

"Well, it survived. It smells like hell," she said, laughing and then starting to cry again. "But it survived. Do you want it?"

Of course. The party was tonight, and if Anne Marie's prediction was true, the woman was still in business, so why not. Anne Marie gave her ten dollars, a fireman retrieved the dress, and Anne Marie went back to work.

Miss Colorado never ceased to amaze Anne Marie. "I thought that was you," she said, when Anne Marie had barely started down the hall. "Did you get the dress?"

"Yes, but something really tragic happened."

"The fire? I know. I heard about it on the news."

If Anne Marie had a TV and hadn't written off the news two years ago when they reported on that little girl being raped and murdered, and showed her little legs sticking out from under the blanket, Anne Marie might have seen the news herself that morning. As it was, she didn't even listen to the radio because they did the news too. That's why she bought the CD player, and Jimmie the CDs, which he took with him, every last one.

"Anne Marie. Anne Marie, dear?"

"Yes?" She looked at Miss Colorado.

"Let me see the dress."

Anne Marie took it out of the bag.

"Oh my," Miss Colorado said, donning her glasses and inspecting it up close, hem and everything. "It'll have to be washed first. It's taking my breath away."

"Mine too," Anne Marie said. "Do you think the material'll be all right?"

Miss Colorado rubbed it between her fingers. "Probably, but I don't know about drying."

"Wonderful," Anne Marie sighed. She'd left work early; she'd had the time coming, but already it was four and the party started at nine.

"Hurry," Miss Colorado said. "Wash it by hand in cold water and take it up to the roof. Go!"

Anne Marie stared. "The roof?"

"Yes, while there's still sun."

Anne Marie washed it in the tub, using a lemon-scented shampoo and conditioner, and draped it over the towel rack to drain while she changed into a pair of shorts and a halter-top. She figured she might as well get a little sun herself, it always had such a therapeutic effect on her, and in passing, glanced at the cactus. At this time of day the sun wouldn't be that bright, maybe it would do the cactus some good also. After all, it sat in direct light on the windowsill at her old place, and had thrived.

She put on her slippers, shook the dress onto a hanger, and with it still dripping, slung it over her shoulder and carefully picked up the cactus. "Don't worry," she assured it, in case it had a memory. "There's an elevator." She rode to the top, backed sideways through a dreary, graffiti-plastered door, and stepped out into another world.

"Wow." She looked around. Apparently this roof was used by sunbathers in the building. There were two chaise loungers on the one side, facing what would be the morning sun, and a hammock under the eaves, with a makeshift table nearby. "Paradise," she said of the view, and found herself going close to the edge to look down. Six floors. She had somewhat of a fear of heights, though not a conventional one. She wasn't afraid of falling; she'd fallen in one form or another all her life. She was afraid of jumping, of being so overwhelmed by the urge, that she'd just up and do it. Jump, jump, jump.

She forced herself to step back and, looking around again, picked the best spot for the cactus and set it down, then tried to figure out what to do with the dress. There was a clothesline and even some clothespins, but the dress was still dripping slightly. At this rate, it would drip for hours, and into the night. She took it off the hanger, shook it again, and twirled around, then around and around, water spraying everywhere, on the cactus, the chaises, the wall. Then side to side. Back and forth. And she felt as if she were dancing. Dancing with a dress, but dancing nonetheless, and it made her laugh.

She thought she heard someone come in the door behind her, and stopped and turned, but no one was there. Her imagination, she thought, and it's a good thing. If someone had seen you, they'd think you were crazy. And if Jimmie had seen you, he'd know.

She hung the dress on the line, checked to make sure the cactus hadn't gotten too wet, checked the splint, and stretched out on one of the chaises. If anyone came up, she'd vacate the premises, since it probably would be theirs, but in the meantime....

"Anne Marie?"

She opened her eyes, felt sleepy, and focused on the man hovering over her, the telephone man. The telephone man? "I personally wouldn't have woke you," he said, "but your neighbor was worried and...."

Anne Marie sat up, glanced quickly at his watch, seven-thirty, and ran her fingers through her hair. "I guess I fell asleep."

"I guess you did," he said, and smiled.

She got up, stepped out and then back into one of her slippers, and hurried over to check the dress. It was almost dry, close enough at least. "I can't believe I fell asleep. I never sleep during the day."

The man shrugged. "Do you need some help," he asked, watching her as she leaned down and picked up the cactus.

"Yes, if you don't mind. Take the dress."

He looked at her. It would make more sense for him to take the cactus, and he reached for it. But she said no. "I don't think it likes men any more."

He laughed, rolling his eyes, as if to say he had a real live one here, and held the door for her. "Is there something wrong with the phones?" Anne Marie asked, when they boarded the elevator and he pressed the button.

"No." He was still in his work clothes.

"What are you doing here then? Do you live around here?"

"No." He glanced at her, and blushed perhaps. She wasn't sure. It's hard to tell when you don't know someone that well, or for that matter at all. "I came to see you," he said. "Didn't your neighbor tell you I stopped by yesterday?"

Anne Marie nodded. "She did, but she didn't say what for. What for?"

He smiled and shook his head. "To see if you wanted to go out or something?"

Anne Marie looked at him, studied his chiseled profile, didn't look at the tattoo, but knew it was there and could see it? "Did you call me the other night?"

"You mean from the truck?"

"No, after that?"

He shook his head, waited for her to step off the elevator, and followed her to her door. "No, you have an unlisted phone number. And yes," he added, when she looked curiously at him. "Even though I technically gave it to you and obviously know it, to call you...well." He shrugged, balanced the cactus for her when it wobbled slightly, and handed her the dress.

"Thank you."

"Have fun tonight," he said.

Anne Marie watched him walk down the hall to the outside door. "Wait a minute. Are you going to call me?"

He turned. "If you want me to."

She smiled. "And you say you know the number?"

"By heart," he said, and was gone.

CHAPTER SEVEN

Miss Colorado put on her glasses and started sewing. "The smell is gone," she said.

"Thank heaven." Anne Marie observed the way she worked, so efficiently, each stitch perfect and evenly placed. "You're amazing."

Miss Colorado smiled. "No, the Flying Walendas were amazing. I was the Incredible."

Anne Marie laughed. "Seriously?"

Miss Colorado nodded, crossed her tiny legs at the ankles, and sewed some more.

"How long's it been since you worked in the circus?"

"Oh, five, six years now."

"Do you miss it?"

Miss Colorado shrugged at first, but then nodded. "I miss the old times, before my eyes went bad."

Anne Marie stared at her, puzzled. "Because...?"

Miss Colorado turned the seam around and started stitching from the opposite end. "Because...." She glanced at Anne Marie with her huge magnified eyes. "I started scaring the children."

Anne Marie hesitated. "Your glasses, you mean?"

Miss Colorado nodded. "One little boy cried, and so did I."

"Wow," Anne Marie said sadly. "I can imagine."

Miss Colorado smiled. "Is your mother proud of you?"

"No, why?"

"Because you're so honest."

"No, actually she hates me for that."

Miss Colorado chuckled. "Just don't go getting pregnant."

"What?"

Miss Colorado held up the dress. "The girl who wore it before you was pregnant."

"How do you know?"

Miss Colorado looked at her, long and hard. "It was let out. Here, see." She showed Anne Marie the alterations. "She was lucky, probably only three or four months. Any more'n that, and...."

Anne Marie pondered the girl's circumstance. "Do you think she did it herself?"

Miss Colorado smiled. "Got pregnant, no. Only one of those that I know of."

Anne Marie laughed. That's not what she'd meant. And Miss Colorado knew that. The two women sobered then.

"I believe so," Miss Colorado said. "But I think she did the best she could."

"I think so too," Anne Marie replied.

"Oh, and why is that?"

"Because she was in love."

Miss Colorado smiled. "Aren't we all at one time."

Anne Marie stared at the dress, imagined the young girl's swollen breasts, and felt her own swell and ache for a second. "Were you ever pregnant, Miss Colorado?"

"No." She shook her head. "I was in love once though, to the man of my dreams...the courageous, the death-defying, the brave, Anton the Lion Tamer."

Anne Marie smiled.

"Oh, what a man."

Anne Marie watched Miss Colorado's eyes grow sad through the depth of her glasses. "What happened to him?"

"He died." She held up the dress. "There now, all done."

Anne Marie thanked her and tried it on. "Perfect."

Miss Colorado felt the sides to see for herself and agreed. "You'll be the belle of the hop."

She wasn't. In fact, not one man asked her to dance. If it weren't for Judy doing the stroll with her each time the band played the crowd favorite, she would've been the ideal fifties wallflower.

"I don't get it," Judy said. All the guys were looking at Anne Marie, looking at her constantly, but not one approached her. "It's like you got the plague or something."

Anne Marie sighed.

"Phil, dance with Anne Marie."

"No thanks," Anne Marie said. She was more annoyed than usual with him tonight. He'd actually had the nerve to honk for her from the road, and then honked again before she even had a chance to grab her purse. "I ache all over anyway."

"I'll bet," Phil said, though he had no idea why, his expression as genuinely puzzled as Anne Marie's and Judy's the minute it came out of his mouth.

"Go get us some punch," Judy told him, and pointed him in the right direction.

"Do you notice everyone looking at me?" Anne Marie asked when he'd gone.

Judy nodded. "I'm jealous. I mean you look good and all, but it's like the guys are practically drooling."

Anne Marie stared. "I feel weird."

"Weird how?"

"I don't know. A little nauseated. How long are we staying?"

Judy watched Phil leave a puddle of punch and then a trail from their three glasses, and sighed. "Not much longer. Another round and he'll start insisting he's okay to drive."

Anne Marie nodded. He was notorious for that.

Her cactus was a welcome sight when she finally returned home, and equally welcome was the silence from the veteran's apartment next door. "'The Lion Sleeps Tonight,'" she sang softly. "In the jungle, the mighty jungle." And it actually felt so good to be home, as soon as she took off her dress and underwear and got into the tub, her nausea passed.

She thought about the telephone man and glanced at the phone, perched as usual on the back of the toilet, and wondered if he'd called while she was gone. Probably not, she decided, since he knew she was going out somewhere. She wondered what he thought about her dress, wondered if he thought it was the kind of thing she wore all the time, probably with her bunny slippers.

Why would he want to call me? A woman like that?

She leaned her head back and let the water dip and crest around her face and ears, and wondered what his name was. When the thought crossed her mind that it might be on the service bill, she got out, wrapped herself in a towel, and went into the kitchen to look. Where had she put it? Where?

In the bread drawer. She didn't like bread in a drawer, not to mention that she hadn't bought any yet. She turned on the light, unfolded the bill, and ran her eyes down over the page.

Danny.

His name was Danny.

Not Dan, not some initial and a last name, the way they listed their names at the Headlands where she worked, but Danny. She liked that.

Danny.

His name was Danny.

CHAPTER EIGHT

Anne Marie woke rested, feeling great, but had no sooner set her feet on the floor, when she became nauseated and had to lie back down. And it wouldn't go away. She had a feeling she could lie there the rest of her life and still be sick to her stomach. So she forced herself to rise, covered her mouth in the event she had to throw up, and headed for the bathroom where, lo and behold, the nausea passed.

"Jesus." She looked at her reflection in the mirror, thought of what Miss Colorado had said, and wished she had a calendar. Her checkbook. She had one in her checkbook. Hurrying to locate it, she counted the weeks she and Jimmie had been apart, added three on top of that because he hadn't had any time for her then, and shook her head. It was impossible, not to mention how she'd practically bled to death for days after he left.

Perhaps it was something she ate, she thought, but dismissed that as well. She hadn't eaten anything. The last thing she'd had was that hot dog on the corner before she got on the bus for the ride home from work, and she always ate that man's hot dogs. She trusted him. Maybe it was because she was hungry. That's it, she thought, low blood sugar. But she was achy all over too, and that made her suspect she was coming down with the flu. She looked at the cactus, sympathized with how it must feel, and planned her day.

Shopping. It was about time she bought groceries, and enough to last two weeks, since that's how often she got paid. She'd better make a list, she decided, because she was always forgetting the most important items, and checked before she left to see if Miss Colorado needed anything.

"No, nothing, dear. Thank you." Miss Colorado asked her about the dance, said she couldn't help but hear how early she'd returned home, and Anne Marie told her all about it, what little there was to tell.

"Are you sure you don't need anything?"

Miss Colorado shook her head.

"So where do I go?" Anne Marie asked.

"Well." Miss Colorado had to think. "There is a supermarket one block over."

Anne Marie looked at her. "Where do you shop?"

Miss Colorado hesitated. "I have my groceries delivered from across town. I don't like going out and it's the only one that...."

Anne Marie understood now. "People stared?"

Miss Colorado nodded. "But it's all right. My only regret is they don't pick and choose. An onion that's soft at the root end is much too strong to eat raw. I tell them and I tell them."

Anne Marie smiled. "I know onions. And if not, I'll learn."

Miss Colorado's distant eyes lit up. "A Vidalia preferably," she said. "Or a Walla Walla or a Texas Sweet. And smell it. Hold it up to your nose."

"Got it."

"If the outer skin smells strong or musty, you don't want it." Miss Colorado leaned out the door as Anne Marie turned to leave. "And be careful, dear. Someone mugged a shopper there last week. I heard it on the news."

No one mugged Anne Marie. In fact, this store was much nicer than where she used to shop for herself and Jimmie. She bought everything on her list, plus two Vidalias for Miss Colorado and one for herself, and returned, carrying just one bag.

Miss Colorado sniffed the onions approvingly, and asked how much they cost.

"Not much," Anne Marie said. She didn't want money to change hands between them. Miss Colorado had refused to charge her for altering the dress, and piddly as some might consider her buying two onions as a way of saying thank you, she wanted to at least do something.

"Per pound I mean."

"Fifty-nine cents, I think."

Miss Colorado nodded, sniffed the onions again, and looked up at her. "You had a visitor while you were gone."

Anne Marie stared. "Really. Who?" she asked, thinking she was going to say the telephone man.

"Your mother."

"My mother?"

"Yes, I told her you'd only be a little while, but she seemed in a hurry."

Anne Marie nodded; her mother was born in a hurry.

"She said to give this to you." Miss Colorado handed her a scribbled note, one Anne Marie didn't exactly have to read to know the gist of what it would say. She had things to do and only a minute to say hi. She'd see her soon. And did she need anything?

"No," Anne Marie said to herself, after she put her groceries away and finally got around to reading the note. "Not a thing." Except maybe the sun, she thought, and at high noon, she headed for the roof. Having decided to take along the cactus again and also a blanket to lie on, just in case, she was glad she had. The chaises were occupied, obviously by their owners, two women about her age, and the one on the inside was definitely a little territorial.

"We're lesbians," she said, with an attitude. "Is that going to bother you?"

"No." Anne Marie shrugged. "I'm nothing. Is that going to bother you?"

The woman's partner smiled, warmly at first, and then with amusement as Anne Marie made her way across the roof lugging the cactus and put it down to check for the right angle of the sun. She moved it three times before settling on a position, turned it so the splint was to the back, and spread out her blanket.

"What's with the cactus?" Miss Congeniality asked.

Anne Marie looked at her. "A man did it," she said, as if that in itself were all that needed to be said. And it sufficed. The two women nodded. Anne Marie stretched out on her stomach then, used her arm as a pillow, and soaked up the sun.

For someone who never napped during the day, she was surprised to find herself yawning and dozing off and on. The two lesbians talked softly between themselves, and from a distance their voices sounded like humming. No, not humming, she thought, more like cooing. When she turned onto her back, she checked the cactus, adjusted it as well, and glanced at them.

32

The not-so-friendly one was rubbing lotion onto the other's shoulder, casually in the beginning, routinely, but then eased her hand down inside her companion's bathing suit top when she noticed Anne Marie watching. Perhaps she wanted to shock Anne Marie; perhaps it was another territorial display. Whatever. But Anne Marie merely yawned and closed her eyes. It didn't move her one way or the other. Sleep. All she wanted to do was sleep. And dream.

CHAPTER NINE

Anne Marie heard a man's voice and opened her eyes.

"Hey, how's it going?" her veteran neighbor asked, making himself at home on the hammock, his apparently, and setting a six-pack on the table next to it.

"Okay," Anne Marie said. "How about you?"

He shrugged and popped open a beer.

The three women exchanged glances from across the expanse of the roof, sad glances, knowing glances, and all felt sorry for him. He seemed oblivious to the hell he raised at night, and his agonizing cries for help.

Anne Marie rested her head back on her arm, made sure her fingers were touching the base of the cactus, and let her mind and eyes wander. The man was very tanned and rather muscular, if you didn't count his swollen stomach. He had a nice face, nice hair too. And big arms, big strong arms. She imagined them pounding on her door, beating it down and him screaming, and shuddered when he gulped down the first beer and started on his second.

She wondered about his family, the way he grew up. Was he a happy child? Did he have nightmares then? Nightmares that came true? She thought of her own, and wondered if his mother told him they were nonsense and to stop crying right now and go back to bed. Or did his mother wrap her arms around him? And did he have a real father?

Beer three, the veteran closed his eyes, and appeared to be happy. Anne Marie denied seeing auras, learned early on it was best to keep her mouth shut about things like that, but saw his aura change for a moment. "What do you mean you see things?" her mother had shouted. "Don't you dare tell anyone that! They'll think you're crazy."

"Am I crazy, Mom?"

"If you keep talking like that, you will be."

The veteran relaxed even more, his strong arms sinking into the hammock, his jaw slackening, and ultimately he showed signs of getting an erection. He smiled inside then; she could see it, smiled all over. But all too quickly, his inner smile faded, along with the diminishing of his erection, and he reached for another beer, then another, downed the rest, and vanished. The lesbians left then too, the friendly one waved. And in time Anne Marie gathered up her blanket and cactus and left as well.

It seems she'd had another visitor in her absence. "I didn't get a good look at him," Miss Colorado said. "I didn't talk to him either."

Anne Marie glanced curiously at her while trying to balance the cactus and unlock the door. "Why?"

Miss Colorado hesitated. "He would have looked at me funny. I can tell."

Jimmie, Anne Marie thought. It had to be Jimmie. But what would he be doing here?

"Do you know how I know?" Miss Colorado said, as if Anne Marie had asked. "When the supermarket delivers my food, it's always a different delivery boy."

Anne Marie gazed at her.

"Your visitor had the same way about him. He was just coming to look."

Anne Marie smiled sadly. "And laugh later?"

Miss Colorado shrugged. "Sometimes they laugh before they even get to the door."

Anne Marie's phone was ringing when she went inside, and rang until she put the cactus down and answered it. "Where have you been?" Judy asked. "I've been trying to get you all day."

Anne Marie lowered the toilet lid and sat on it. "I've been getting some sun. Why?"

"Phil lost his job."

Anne Marie stared at the tub. "How?" Phil was always losing his job.

"He got fired. Someone said he took something."

Anne Marie nodded. He was always taking something too. "What did he take this time?"

"Anne Marie!"

"All right. What did they say he took?"

"I don't know, it doesn't matter. He didn't take it, so who cares?"

Anne Marie watched a tiny spider make its way up and out of the tub drain and thought of The Itsy Bitsy Spider nursery rhyme, and then the song about the little old ant trying to move a rubber-tree plant. "Anyone knows an ant can't...move a rubber tree plant."

Judy chuckled. "What's that got to do with it?"

Anne Marie smiled, helped the spider along by nudging it when it reached about halfway up the side and kept slipping back on little drops of water, and considered what she was supposed to say, what her mother might say. "Do you guys need anything? Is there anything I can do to help?"

"As a matter of fact, yes," Judy said. "Phil wants a good job this time. He says he's tired of working in sales."

Sales? Phil worked the night shift in a convenience store.

"He wants to know if you know of any good jobs."

Anne Marie stared; the spider was back. "Tell him to look in the paper."

"He did. He says they're not for him."

"Wait a minute, I think there's something wrong with my phone. It's making a noise."

"It's probably call waiting."

"What?"

"Call waiting. Click over."

"How?"

"Press the receiver."

"What?"

"Just press it and say hello."

Anne Marie hesitated, pressed the button, and held her breath. "Hello."

"Anne Marie?"

"Yes."

"It's Danny. The man who...."

Anne Marie got up off the toilet seat. "Hi."

"Hi."

A momentary silence ensued. "How are you?" he asked.

"Fine," she said. "I didn't know I had call waiting? How do I get back?"

"Press the receiver."

"Will you hold on?"

"Yeah, I'll be here."

"Is this free?"

"For a month."

"Good. Hold on." Anne Marie pressed down on the receiver as if it would bite and ventured another hello.

"Who called?" Judy asked.

"The telephone man. I gotta go."

"What? What telephone man? What does he want?"

"He wants to talk. I'll call you later. He has a tattoo." Anne Marie switched back before Judy could say anything else and once again offered a tentative hello.

"So," Danny, the telephone man said. "How was the party?"

Anne Marie had to think. Since it didn't actually feel like a party to her, she'd all but forgotten it. "Okay I guess. The band wasn't bad."

"Do you feel like doing something tonight?"

Anne Marie hesitated, stared at the toilet and had to pee, but decided to hold it. Tonight? What kind of man, she could hear her mother say, calls up a woman at five o'clock on a Saturday and asks do you want to do something tonight? What kind of man...? "Like what?" Anne Marie asked.

"I don't know, a movie maybe, dinner."

"Sure," Anne Marie said. Why not?

"I'll pick you up around seven. How's that?"

"Fine," she said, crossing her legs. "I'll see you then."

CHAPTER TEN

Jimmie returned. Anne Marie was drying her hair and didn't hear him knock, but Miss Colorado assured her it was the same person. "I just thought you might want to know."

"Thank you."

Miss Colorado focused her distant eyes on her. "Are you going out?"

"Yes, with the telephone man."

Miss Colorado nodded and smiled. "I knew he'd be back."

Anne Marie blushed, didn't know herself, but had hoped. "He seems nice."

Miss Colorado shrugged. "He called you inconsiderate, remember."

"He didn't know me then."

"And he knows you now?"

Anne Marie laughed. "No, but I set him straight."

He'd be arriving in about half an hour.

"You're nervous," Miss Colorado said. "Come have some tea."

Anne Marie said she'd love to, but should probably stay put in the event he came early. "Don't worry, I'll hear him," Miss Colorado said, and Anne Marie smiled. Of course she would.

"What kind of tea is this?" Anne Marie asked, sipping the brew, steeped to perfection.

"Green tea with a touch of ginger."

"It's delicious. Is it magic?"

Miss Colorado smiled. "A potion you mean, dear?"

Anne Marie nodded. "I feel so calm."

Miss Colorado's smile widened on her tiny little face.

"Tell me more about the circus," Anne Marie said. "What did you like most about it?"

"Well," Miss Colorado drew a breath and sighed. "Besides Anton, there was Minerva."

Anne Marie pondered the name, tried to picture an act surrounding it.

"She was an elephant."

Anne Marie stared. "An elephant?"

"A white elephant, in every sense of the word."

"What do you mean?"

"She refused to do tricks."

"Wow. What did they do with her?"

"I don't know."

"Was there something wrong with her?"

"Oh no. She was the sweetest elephant. She would bow when no one was there and look at you with her big eyes, and she would touch you so lightly, it was like a feather."

Anne Marie shook her head. "I don't understand."

"She was a gift from a zoo."

"A gift."

"Yes. See, she'd given birth, but couldn't give milk. It was very rare in those days for a captive elephant to give birth."

"How sad."

Miss Colorado nodded. "To give life and not be able to sustain it...."

"Did you take care of her?"

"As long as I could?"

"What do you mean?"

"I was sold."

"You were what?"

"Sold, dear." She put her cup and saucer down. "Your telephone man is here."

No, Anne Marie thought, not now, and went out rather reluctantly to greet him. "Danny."

He turned, a little startled, and smiled. "Hi."

She told Miss Colorado good-bye, pulled the door closed behind her, and walked across the hall. "I just need to get my purse."

He smiled again, followed her, and stood just inside to wait. "So where did you decide we're going?" she asked from the bedroom, where a sudden wave of nausea came over her. Eat, I need to eat.

"I don't know. I thought I'd leave that up to you."

She stared at the pink taffeta hanging in her closet, felt another wave of nausea, and couldn't help but think again about the pregnant young girl. It was then, and holding her own stomach for fear she was about to throw up, that a more urgent feeling came over her. A feeling of panic. Of having to run hard, as fast as she could. And far.

"Oh my God...." She turned toward the door, took one step and crumbled to the floor. "Danny," she gasped. "Danny."

"What?"

Silence.

"Anne Marie?" He waited a second or two, hesitated still, called her name again, and went to investigate.

"What the...?" She lay on the floor. He rushed in, felt her wrist for a pulse, and scooped her up into his arms and laid her on the bed. "Anne Marie? Anne Marie, wake up!"

When she didn't respond, he hurried into the bathroom, ran cold water on a washcloth, and rushed back and pressed it to her forehead. "Anne Marie...come on, wake up," he said. "Wake up." She looked dead. Beautiful and bronze, but dead.

The reality of the situation hit him all at once. He hardly knew her, he's in the bedroom with her, and she's lying dead. "Oh Christ." He left the washcloth on her forehead, took off across the hall, and pounded on Miss Colorado's door.

She didn't answer.

"Please," he said, frantically. "It's your neighbor Anne Marie. She's...."

The doorknob turned.

"I think she's fainted," he told her. "Is she diabetic? Do you know?"

Miss Colorado shook her tiny head. "No!" She grabbed hold of the telephone man's arm. "Take me to her."

He led her across the hall and into Anne Marie's bedroom, where she felt the young woman's face, pressed her ear to her beating heart, and gazed blindly around the room. "Look for a syringe. Look for anything."

Danny started searching. "I think we should call 911," he said, combing her dresser, the windowsill, her closet.... He even searched under her pillows for some reason, and then slid his hand up under the mattress, where all he found was a pair of underwear.

It was then Anne Marie stirred and opened her eyes, saw Miss Colorado, and started apologizing. "Why are you crying? What's the matter? Why are you crying?"

The tiny woman wiped at her eyes, squeezed Anne Marie's hand, and gave the washcloth to the telephone man. Anne Marie noticed him standing there then, a frantic look on his face, and with a pair of her panties in his hand. In a flash he disappeared.

"Here." He returned with the fresh washcloth and handed it to Miss Colorado.

"Get me out of here," Anne Marie said. "I need to sit up."

Danny reached down instinctively, scooped her into his arms again, Miss Colorado held onto her hand, and they went into the living room, where seated, Anne Marie started breathing easier. "Oh my God, that was weird," she said. "Really weird."

"Are you diabetic?" Danny asked.

She shook her head, noticed again how he stood holding her pair of underwear in his hand, and closed her eyes.

"Anne Marie?" Miss Colorado and Danny both feared she was slipping again. "Anne Marie?"

"I'm fine," she said. "I'm fine." And she was fine. Whatever it was had passed, and soon she was talking, as her mother would say, a mile a minute. "How'd you get over here?" she asked Miss Colorado. "Are you all right?"

Miss Colorado nodded, and it was then Danny headed for the bathroom, where looking around for a clothes hamper or basket, (there was none) he put her underwear on top of the medicine cabinet and splashed cold water on his face.

When he returned, he sat down on the windowsill next to the cactus and drew a deep breath. "I need my purse," Anne Marie told him, hesitant to go back into the bedroom to get it herself. "It's on my dresser."

He looked at her. Was she serious? Did she think after all that, they were still going to go out? He shook his head.

"I'm fine," she insisted, and walked Miss Colorado back across the hall. "I won't be late," she said, and Miss Colorado nodded.

"He's the one," she whispered to Anne Marie. "He's the one."

"The one what?"
"The one in your cards."
"My cards?"
Danny appeared at her side. "Are you sure you still want to...?"
"Yes," Anne Marie said.
And thus, their date began.

CHAPTER ELEVEN

Danny drove an '81 Camaro Z28 that he rebuilt and restored himself. He said it took him two years from start to finish, part-time, and Anne Marie imagined him putting it together piece by piece with model airplane glue, first the chassis, then the fenders, then the wheels.

"It's beautiful."

He opened the door for her and before walking around and getting in behind the wheel, fastened her into the seat belt. "It doesn't always work right," he said. It wasn't used that often and sometimes didn't latch completely.

She looked at his tattoo, and then at his hands. They were trembling. "Are you all right?" she asked.

He nodded, and glanced at her. "Do you do that kind of thing often?"

"No, that was the first time."

He waited for her to elaborate. She didn't, so he started the engine and pulled onto the road. The car had a nice sound, even to Anne Marie, who didn't know a whole lot about how cars were supposed to sound, and she commented on it.

He looked at her at the light, smiled an appreciative smile, and asked her what she wanted to do. "I don't know," she said. She wasn't one to go to a movie and didn't even know what was playing, but was hungry, so....

"Why don't we eat first," she suggested.

"Okay, where would you like to go?"

"I don't know." The last time she ate out was over a year ago, unless you count all the Happy-Hours Jimmie used to like to frequent. "Onion rings sound nice."

He smiled. "Onion rings?"

She nodded. "Onion rings, a burger, and a chocolate milk shake."

"Okay." He laughed. "I know just the place." He glanced in his rearview mirror, made a U-turn, and headed in the opposite direction.

He took her to an old fashioned diner, a favorite haunt for muscle-car owners. "Why do they call them that?" she asked, when they pulled in and parked.

"I don't know," Danny said, and speculated. "Men showing off, flexing their muscles and horsepower I guess."

Anne Marie smiled when she noticed one being driven by a woman.

"Come on, let's go inside. You've got to see this place." It was as authentic as could be. Swivel stools at the counter, booths with individual jukebox players, checkerboard linoleum floor, soda fountain, and lots of noise from the kitchen.

"Number five!" shouted the cook as he banged on a bell.

"Wow." Anne Marie looked around and felt right at home. She even had an urge to go check her hair in the ladies room and put on lipstick, odd in itself, since her hair was never one of her major concerns and she never wore lipstick.

"Let's sit over there," Danny said, motioning to an open booth by the window.

"Do you come here a lot?" Anne Marie asked, when they were seated across from one another.

"Not really," he said, and someone called to him then. He waved, smiled, and here came the man with a woman in tow.

"How the hell are you?"

"Fine," Danny said. "How about you two?"

Danny introduced them. The man's name was Joe, and his wife's, Rose. And since they'd brought their drinks along, obviously intending to join them, Danny moved around and sat next to Anne Marie.

"I was Danny's best man," Joe said, which brought an apparent swift kick from his wife under the table. "What? They're divorced now. What's the big deal?"

Rose rolled her eyes apologetically at Anne Marie, and Anne Marie smiled.

"What'll it be?" a waitress asked, pen and pad in hand.

Danny glanced at Anne Marie to see if she'd changed her mind, she hadn't, and he ordered the same for both of them.

"How sweet," Joe said. Another kick. "So how long have you two been dating?"

Danny turned to Anne Marie when she looked at him, the very first time they actually really, really, looked into one another's eyes, and they both smiled. "We met a couple of weeks ago," Danny said.

Anne Marie liked his answer, and also the way he changed the subject. While Joe's "shit-ass" carburetor was discussed, she surprised herself by knowing every word of a song playing on the jukebox, which she would swear she'd never heard before, and leafed through the rest of the selections.

When Danny handed her two quarters, she picked one song and let Rose pick the other. Rose's played first, an early Beatles' tune, and then Anne Marie's.

"Oh, I love that song," Rose said. It was "Tell Laura I Love Her." And sure enough, though Anne Marie knew the words to this song as well, like the woman at the vintage shop said, she definitely had the second line of the chorus wrong. It wasn't "Tell Laura I didn't leave her." It was "Tell Laura I need her." And yet every time that line was sung....

Danny looked at her, noticed something about her. "Are you okay?" he asked.

"I'm fine," she said, and was grateful when the food arrived.

Joe and Rose sat with them until they were done eating, then said they had to leave to go check on their two-year old, who was with a babysitter and in his first week of potty-training. "What a trip," Joe said, marveling over how the little guy was fighting them every step of the way, saying that he didn't like to poop. "Can you believe that?" Once again, Rose kicked him under the table.

"It was nice meeting you, Anne Marie," she said.

"It was nice meeting you too."

When she and Danny were alone again, he returned to his seat opposite her and shrugged, as if to apologize for Joe as well.

Anne Marie smiled.

"What's your favorite song?" he asked, nodding toward the jukebox and fishing into his pocket for more change.

"Oh, I don't know. C7 I guess."

"Which is...?"

Anne Marie stared. She didn't know. Not only that, she didn't know why she'd said it. It certainly wasn't like her to be spontaneous. All anyone had to do was ask Jimmie about that. She found herself leafing back through the selections to find it, and hesitated. She'd never heard of it before.

"'Walking to New Orleans.'"

"Wow," she muttered, and listened to the words. "Well, now ain't that a shame..." she sang along in her mind. "You're the one to blame...."

She looked at Danny. "I guess I do know it," she said, and he smiled.

"What?" she asked, from the way he was smiling.

He shook his head. "It *is* nice meeting you, Anne Marie."

She didn't know what to say, and for a moment, the two of them just looked at one another again. Then the song ended and it seemed a good time to leave. Danny motioned for the check, paid and left a tip, and they walked outside.

CHAPTER TWELVE

Danny fastened Anne Marie into her seat belt again, but made a joke about it, saying she was on her own after this and to be sure to listen for the snap, and Anne Marie told him not to worry. He turned the radio on low.

"So where to now?"

Anne Marie hesitated. She didn't know. "Is there a circus in town?"

Danny laughed. Even if there was, it would be closed by now. "I don't think so. What else?"

Anne Marie thought for a moment. "Do you want to just drive around?"

Danny looked at her.

"I don't get to ride in a car that often," she said, particularly not a car like this, where you see the stars through the roof. She searched for the Big Dipper, found it, and was so mesmerized by the vastness of the night, she didn't notice the way Danny gazed at her.

"Do you want the T-tops out?"

She looked at him.

"The T-tops," he said. "They come out. Do you want them out?"

She smiled. "Yes."

The night opened up even more then; the sky at times seeming close enough to touch, and she thought of her grandmother Light's reverence for the moon. "Pay attention," she'd say.

"But what if it's cloudy?" Anne Marie had asked.

"It doesn't matter. A woman feels the moon inside. A woman is the moon inside."

"Nonsense," Anne Marie's mother said. "The only thing a woman feels inside is pain, and if that's the moon...."

"Anne Marie."

She looked at Danny.

"I used to live right there," he said, pointing to a small bungalow with a white picket fence.

Anne Marie smiled. "Who lives there now?"

He shrugged. "I don't know."

"Where are your parents?"

He glanced into his rearview mirror. "They moved to Florida."

Anne Marie nodded. The great migration. Her mother was talking about moving. "Do you get along with your family?"

"So so," he said.

Anne Marie looked at him, a man she hardly knew, and yet.... "Do you miss them?"

Danny hesitated. "No, if anything I miss my brother."

"Did he move too?"

"No, he died."

"I'm sorry."

He smiled, a smile that said it's okay, to the extent that there was nothing he could do about it, and downshifted to start up a hill.

Anne Marie glanced at the tattoo on his arm, noticed the way it caught the reflection of the streetlights, and leaned her head back.

"Grandmother?"

"Yes."

"What's it mean?"

"It means...."

"Look," Danny said.

Anne Marie focused, and then smiled. An elderly man and woman were walking arm-in-arm down the sidewalk with two little poodles trailing behind them on leashes. An odd enough sight at this almost midnight hour, let alone the fact that the couple were wearing glow in the dark jogging suits and moving at a clipped pace.

"Where are we?" Anne Marie asked, half expecting him to say Mars, they'd been climbing and climbing for so long.

"Dembo Heights," he said.

Anne Marie nodded, she'd heard of it, and realized how far she was from home. She turned and looked over her shoulder to see the couple again, but only saw them disappear before her eyes. She glanced at Danny, wanted to ask if he'd seen them disappear too, but knew better. Jimmie used to hate it when she'd say things like that.

"Just don't! Okay, Anne? Just don't!"

She settled back and started humming an old fifties tune. "To know, know, know him, is to love, love, love him."

Danny smiled.

"He's the one," she could hear Miss Colorado say.

"The one what?"

Danny pulled off the road at a turnaround and parked. "Come on," he said. "There's something I want to show you."

They got out and walked down a tree-lined path, ducking here and there. Danny held the branches back for her as they stepped into a small clearing.

"Oh my," Anne Marie said, edging closer. They were seemingly miles above the city, on the other side of the river although she didn't remember crossing a bridge, with a panoramic view of the city lights. "Wow!"

"Awesome, isn't it?" Danny said.

Anne Marie nodded. It all but took her breath away. "Did you ever wonder what it would be like to fly?" she asked.

Danny smiled. "Not lately," he said, and Anne Marie laughed. It was nice laughing so close to the edge.

"What *do* you think about, Danny?"

He hesitated, gazing at her in the moonlight. "Well, lately I've been thinking about you."

Anne Marie looked at him. That too was nice. They heard a train whistle then and searched for its origin, which turned out to be a lone locomotive, and watched it snake its way along the river bank until it was out of sight.

"We'd better get going," Danny said, and they walked back to the car. "Are you cold?"

"No, I'm fine," Anne Marie said, and couldn't have felt better, no aches and pains for a change, no worries. She'd been enjoying herself. And likewise, with hardly any cars on the road, the ride home was even nicer. Danny pointed out different landmarks as they cruised along. She liked watching him shift gears, liked the way the engine rumbled whenever he slowed to a stop. And she liked the way he laughed. When they pulled up and parked in front of her apartment building, she hated to see the night end. But she didn't show it.

Her mother said, "Never, I mean ever, show a man...."

Danny walked her to her door. The building was quiet.

"I had a good time, Anne Marie," he said. "Thanks for...."

Anne Marie stopped listening to the voices in her head and nodded. "Me too."

"Can I call you again?"

"Yes," she said. And when she smiled, he leaned down and kissed her lightly. "Good night."

He waited for her to unlock her door and go inside, to make sure she was safe and secure, and walked back out to his car. Anne Marie watched from her window as he got in, and when he looked at her, waved. He hesitated then, smiled, and she watched him drive away.

CHAPTER THIRTEEN

Anne Marie checked the cactus and was headed into the bedroom to change, when a sudden wave of nausea washed over her. And a lightheadedness. A whole tidal wave of it, right in the face. She tried to steady herself. Anxiety; it's just anxiety. That's all. Don't panic.

She staggered to the couch, sat down gingerly, and drew a couple of deep breaths. Her mother said as a child she suffered from anxiety attacks all the time. She said it used to embarrass her to death.

"Don't panic. Don't panic," she told herself, and for once she didn't. She remained calm, the nausea passed, and her head cleared. Just like that. "Wow!"

I won't push it, she thought. I'll stay right here. But that wouldn't do, she had to go to the bathroom. She waited another minute or so, stood hesitantly, and went in to use the toilet, and felt fine. She washed her face and brushed her teeth then and looked in the mirror. Studying her reflection, she wondered what Danny saw in her, and if he saw anything. Did he see...?

She heard a noise and froze, a swishing noise. Then heard it again. Rustling. What was that? A mouse, she told herself. Maybe it's just a mouse. Or a rat. Oh my God. A rat? She turned, didn't want to hear it again, jumped when the backs of her legs brushed the tub, and slammed the door shut. Whatever it was, could stay out there.

She grabbed all the towels she had, three, and all the washcloths, four not counting the wet one on the sink, pushed the rug against the bottom crack of the door, and crawled into the tub. She'd stay in here and check the apartment tomorrow. Now, if she could only get comfortable with the washcloths as a pillow and the towels as sheets and a blanket. The phone rang and she jumped again, banging both elbows on the sides of the tub, her crazy bones, and the pain and insanity reverberated to her brain.

"You have no brain," she could hear Jimmie say, "just this big empty space." This the same day he told her she worried too much and analyzed things too much. "Now go to sleep."

"I can't, Jimmie. I can't."

She grabbed the phone. "Hello."

"Anne Marie. This is your mother."

"What?" Anne Marie glanced at her wrist to see what time it was, but didn't wear a watch, and hadn't since she was a kid and her Mickey Mouse broke. "What's the matter?"

"Nothing. I'm in the hospital."

Nothing? Nothing, like the nothing the night her father left? "Why? What happened?"

Her mother hesitated. "I um...." The woman drew a deep breath. "I'm having surgery in the morning."

"What? When?"

"At eight."

"For what?"

"A hysterectomy. The doctor found a mass and.... They say it's probably nothing."

Nothing, nothing, nothing. Anne Marie wanted to scream. "Did you get a second opinion?"

Her mother hesitated again. "No. With my schedule, I just...."

She didn't have the time. She didn't want to waste the time. Almighty time. "Which hospital?"

"Lutheran General."

Anne Marie nodded, she should have known. "Do you want me to come down?"

"No, that's not necessary," her mother said, clearing her throat. "Like I said, the doctor says it's nothing."

"Then why operate?"

Her mother sighed. "I don't know. I just wanted you to know. All right?"

Of course. Anne Marie curled up into a ball in the tub.

"I'll call you tomorrow."

Anne Marie nodded. "I don't think you should do it, Mom," she said. But it was too late. Her mother had already hung up.

Anne Marie eventually fell asleep, but woke repeatedly to hear rustling outside the door, back and forth, back and forth. Swish,

swish. Swish, swish. And couldn't stand it anymore. She reached for the phone and dialed the time. Please let it be morning, she kept thinking, as it rang and rang. Please....

"At the tone, the time will be four forty-three."

She pictured herself cramped in the tub another hour or two till daylight, and cringed. Lutheran General was clear across town and the buses didn't start until six. But then again, if she started walking now.... She got up out of the tub, ached all over, and peed and peed and peed, combed her hair, and mustered up the courage to open the door. She didn't have time to change, not if she were going to get there before eight. She grabbed her purse off the couch without daring to look around, and started out.

It was raining, just a steady drizzle, but rain nonetheless, and took its toll after the ninth or tenth block. She was drenched and shivering when she finally entered the lobby of the hospital, her vision a blur, and quite a sight.

"Miss?" a woman behind the desk said. "Are you all right?"

She nodded, unaware she'd been crying since 52nd Street. "I'm here to see my mother. She's having surgery."

"What's her name?"

"Rebecca Light."

The woman checked a list, found the name, and pointed her in the right direction. "You'd better hurry. They may have taken her down already. She's in Room 310."

Anne Marie thanked her, rode the elevator to the third floor, and wiped her eyes as she started down the hall. There were nurses everywhere.

"Three-ten? It's just down there."

Anne Marie approached the room warily and hesitated outside the door. She could hear her mother's voice, what she thought was her mother's voice, but then wasn't so sure.

"I was hoping my daughter would come."

Another woman, apparently a nurse, sympathized. "Oh, you know how children are these days. It's not that they don't care, it's just that they're always so busy."

"Perhaps," she heard a version of her mother's voice saying, a version she couldn't ever remember hearing before today. Her mother was scared. Her mother was crying.

"Can I help you?" an aide in the hall asked.

Anne Marie looked at her. "No, no thank you." She couldn't go in there. Her mother would die if Anne Marie saw her crying. She'd die. "I'm sorry. I guess I have the wrong floor." She hurried back down the hall, pressed the elevator button, and turned to see her mother being wheeled right toward her on a gurney. "Oh my God," she muttered, and wiped her eyes dry.

"Hold the door please," the nurse said.

Anne Marie nodded. "Mom?"

Her mother turned her head. "Anne Marie?"

"I'm sorry," Anne Marie said, backing up and making room. "I just got here."

"You didn't have to come. I told you, you didn't have to come."

"I know."

The nurse glanced from one to the other.

"Are you all right?" Anne Marie asked.

Her mother nodded. "They gave me something. I'm starting to feel it."

"Press two," the nurse said.

Anne Marie pressed the button, stepped back against the wall as the doors closed, and barely had time to draw a breath before they were opening again. "Mom, are you sure you want to...?"

"Yes," her mother said drowsily. "Not everyone dies in surgery, Anne Marie. Don't let your imagination run away with you." She was wheeled across the threshold of surgery then, eyes closed, and was gone.

Grandmother Light died in surgery.

"Miss?"

Anne Marie turned and stared at a nurse from a different time. A solemn woman in a stern habit. "The family waiting room is just down the hall. You'll have to follow me."

CHAPTER FOURTEEN

Miss Colorado passed Anne Marie a cup of tea. "Drink," she said.

Anne Marie nodded, teeth chattering as she took a sip.

"Drink some more."

Anne Marie forced another mouthful down. The tea was bitter, very bitter. "It's supposed to be," Miss Colorado said. And strong. Anne Marie was no longer soaking wet, but chilled to the bone, and weak. Her mother's surgery had taken four hours, due to unforeseen hemorrhaging, and nothing turned into something.

"Cancer?"

The surgeon fixed his eyes on her. "Didn't your mother tell you?"

Anne Marie shook her head.

"Well, we think we got it all, so let's be positive. We have her sedated, so you might as well go on home."

"Would it be all right to see her first?"

"Yes, but only for a minute."

"How was she?" Miss Colorado asked.

"Asleep." Anne Marie thought about the death glow surrounding the doctor, how it followed him down the hall. "They said she'd be out of it most of the day."

Miss Colorado nodded. "Finish your tea."

Anne Marie drank what was left and sat back, feeling rather tingly all over. Miss Colorado asked specific questions then. Anne Marie had answers for each, since they were the same questions she'd asked. And in time, exhausted, Anne Marie started to relax. She thanked Miss Colorado for the tea and for listening, and stood up to leave.

She hesitated. "Miss Colorado, do you mind if...?"

The tiny woman looked at her.

"Do you mind if I ask you something?"

Miss Colorado shrugged.

"You said you were sold. Who sold you?"

Miss Colorado paused. "Well, the first time," she said, "it was my father."

The first time? Anne Marie stared.

"That time wasn't so bad. I wanted to get away, so...."

Anne Marie suddenly wished she hadn't asked.

"The second time...." Miss Colorado raised her shoulders in a helpless gesture. "It was the ringmaster. I wasn't holding my own, he said. He said I had no talent."

Anne Marie shook her head in disbelief.

"That's when I learned to juggle. And to sew. And to read cards and tea leaves. And to care for the animals. And to mix cures. And to...."

"Were you ever sold again?"

Miss Colorado nodded and then laughed. "Yes, once more. But this time it was because I'd learned to do so very much."

Anne Marie shook her head again. "How sad."

"No, not really, not at this point. You see, because that was when I met Anton."

Anne Marie thought about what she said as she walked back across the hall and into her own apartment, and had no sooner stepped inside her bedroom when a familiar wave of nausea came over her.

"No," she cried. "I'm not going to do this. No!" Fight it, fight it, she told herself. But nausea had its way. She hurried into the bathroom, felt for sure this time she was going to throw up, but just like yesterday, once there and clutching the toilet, the nausea passed.

Her bedroom, she decided, it had to be her bedroom. Something in there was making her sick. Something dead. Mice, rats.... Gas. A gas leak. What if it is a gas leak? "Oh Lord!" She quickly dialed the Super.

"A boiler? No gas?"

"You have baseboard heat," he said.

She stared, wondering again what it could be.

"I'll come take a look," the man said, and showed up about ten minutes later.

"In there." Anne Marie pointed. Just looking in that direction was enough to bring on nausea now, so she waited by the cactus.

"I'm sorry, ma'am," he said, emerging after a thorough search. "I can't find anything. In fact, it smells rather nice in there, kinda lemony."

"Lemony?" Anne Marie looked at the man.

"Yeah, lemony," he said.

Anne Marie thanked him and apologized for bothering him.

"It was no bother," he said. "Anytime."

Anne Marie followed him to the door.

"If there's anything I can do to help, you just let me know."

Anne Marie nodded and smiled. The man looked like Robert Redford on a good day. "Thanks again."

When he left, she turned toward the bedroom. This was obviously just her imagination, as her mother would say, and she'd just have to deal with it. The smell of lemon never made her nauseated before.

"But you weren't pregnant before," a voice in her head said.

What?

Nothing.

Pregnant? Not me. I can't be. I had my period.

"You menstruated," a different voice said.

"All right." It was her grandmother's. "I menstruated."

She walked out into the hall and knocked on Miss Colorado's door. "Can you tell me if I'm pregnant," she asked.

Miss Colorado peered at her. "I'm not sure."

"What do you mean?"

"Sometimes when you speak...."

Anne Marie sighed. "Never mind. Thank you."

Miss Colorado called after her. "They do have tests you know, if you want to be sure."

Anne Marie's face lit up. "What kind of test?"

"Urine tests, at the drug store. I hear them advertised on TV."

Anne Marie nodded and smiled, she thought she'd meant....

"Of course if it's a reading you want."

"Yes."

"Come see me later then. After the sun goes down."

Anne Marie hesitated. "Why then?"

"Because the moon'll be out."

Anne Marie should have known. "Do I have to prepare in any way?"

"No," Miss Colorado said. "Come just as you are."

Anne Marie had hours to kill. She drew a bath, stripped, and climbed in and settled back. When the phone rang, it was her mother. "I'm fine. Don't bother coming down. I'm going back to sleep."

A few minutes later the phone rang again, and it was Judy this time. "What's he like? What's he like? What's he like?"

"Who?"

"Your telephone man."

"Oh." Anne Marie smiled. She hadn't forgotten him. She'd just tucked him safely away, behind a door in the recesses of her mind. "He's nice."

"Nice? That's it?"

Anne Marie smiled, told her a little about the date, and then about her mother.

"No kidding? Is she all right?"

"I guess." Anne Marie didn't speculate on the outcome, said she was going to visit her tomorrow after work, and that she had to go now, because the water was getting cold.

"Speaking of work, that reminds me."

Anne Marie cringed.

"Please find something for Phil."

Anne Marie sighed, and while staring at the ceiling in frustration over how a friend would ask something she knew deep down was wrong, she suddenly noticed her underwear on top of the medicine cabinet; the same pair Danny had in his hands when she woke last night from fainting. The same pair that had laid at his feet when he was a perfect stranger. There they were again. She shook her head and laughed.

"What's so funny?" Judy asked.

"Nothing."

"I'll call you tomorrow."

Anne Marie hung up and sobered. It was one thing for Danny to want to take her out even though she wore an old prom dress and bunny slippers and left her underwear everywhere. But pregnant?

He'd be gone in a minute, and rightfully so, she thought. She'd be linked to Jimmie for the rest of her life then...and the poor little baby would be too.

CHAPTER FIFTEEN

"What are you wearing, dear?" Miss Colorado asked, furrowing her brow and touching the fabric.

"A toga," Anne Marie said. "Well, actually it's just a sheet, but...."

Miss Colorado smiled, bade her to sit down, and doing so under the scrutiny of her distant eyes, Anne Marie felt compelled to explain. There is nothing worse, her grandmother used to say, than misunderstanding. "This nausea I keep feeling only seems to happen when I go into my bedroom, so I thought...."

Miss Colorado nodded. Her linen closet, like Anne Marie's, was off the hall this side of the bathroom. "Well, it's just lovely, I can tell."

Anne Marie laughed. "I feel like Claudius."

"Oh? And not Cleopatra?"

"No."

Miss Colorado reached for the teapot and poured hot water over the Oolong leaves in both their cups. "Are you sure you want to know?"

"Yes," Anne Marie said, and thought of her grandmother again. "Tell me. Tell me everything," she used to say to her. And her grandmother's face would always change then, one side happy, one side sad. "Tell me everything."

Miss Colorado smiled, grew solemn as they waited for the leaves to settle, then nodded. It was time. "Drink. Drink, so that we may know. Drink," she said, "so that you may know."

Anne Marie drank all but a swallow, swirled the remaining tea counter-clockwise three times, and turned the cup upside down on the saucer before placing it in Miss Colorado's child-sized hands.

"There now." Miss Colorado waited another moment, then turned it upright and used a magnifying glass to peer inside. "Let's see what we have."

Anne Marie lowered her eyes to her lap.

"There is a baby."

Anne Marie looked up.

"But so low in the cup."

Anne Marie stared.

"Do you want to see?"

Anne Marie shook her head.

"This would have been a long time ago. A very long time ago. You are how old, dear?"

"Twenty-six," Anne Marie said. "But there was no long time ago for me. I've only known Jimmie that way."

Miss Colorado nodded and resumed reading. "It was a girl."

Anne Marie stared.

"A little baby girl."

Laura, Anne Marie thought, like the song, 'Tell Laura I love her.' Tell Laura I didn't leave her.

"I see your dress," Miss Colorado said. "Your prom dress."

"It's not my prom dress. I never went to the prom."

Miss Colorado put her magnifying glass down.

"What?"

She hesitated.

"Tell me."

Miss Colorado paled. "There's death."

"The baby?"

"I don't know." Tears sprang to her eyes. "The answer lies in you."

"Me? Why me?"

Miss Colorado shook her head and dabbed her eyes. "I don't know. It's not good though. It's not good."

Anne Marie apologized for upsetting her and tried to comfort her, to no avail. "Wait a minute, I'll be right back." It had to be the dress, there was no other explanation. No other connection. She'd go and get it and they'd find out once and for all and put it to rest.

"I keep thinking of Minerva," Miss Colorado said, as Anne Marie started out. "How they said she cried real tears when they took her babies away."

Anne Marie looked back from the door. "Were any of them named Laura?"

Miss Colorado gazed blindly in her direction, appeared stunned for a moment, and then laughed. Anne Marie was so unpretentious it was a delight. "No, I don't think so."

Anne Marie headed across the hall, heard someone to her right, and stopped. It was Danny. "Danny?"

He looked at her as if seeing a mirage and she suddenly realized why. The toga. "What are you doing here?" she asked. She didn't need a man present when she was calling upon the moon. "Go away," she wanted to say. "Go away." But then he smiled that smile of his.

"I was worried about you," he said. "I've been calling you all day."

"I've been in and out," Anne Marie said. "Can you do me a favor?"

He nodded somewhat warily. "Why are you wearing a sheet?"

Anne Marie looked at him, feigning indignance. "It's a toga."

"Oh really?" Again Danny smiled. "It looks like a sheet to me."

"Who's there?" Miss Colorado asked, peering out her door.

"It's Danny," Anne Marie said.

"The telephone man?"

"Yes."

Danny said, "Hi."

Miss Colorado said hello and asked if Anne Marie was still coming back.

"Yes, I'll be right there."

She led Danny over to her apartment, unlocked the door, and pointed to her bedroom. "Could you go in my closet and get me that pink prom dress?"

He looked at her. "Why?"

"Because I think it's what's making me sick."

Danny just looked at her again. "The dress?"

She nodded. "Get it and bring it to me slowly."

Danny laughed. "All right, but you'd better not faint on me again. Because if you do, I'm outta here."

Anne Marie stopped him. "Wait. What if I do faint?"

Danny paused and sighed. "Just in case, go sit down." He pointed to the couch, shook his head at the sight of her sitting there wrapped in a sheet waiting to faint, and went in to get the dress.

Anne Marie looked up when he reentered the living room, dress in hand. So far so good. When she nodded, he came closer, and then closer. Nothing. No nausea, no lightheadedness, no fear. She motioned for him to lay the dress in her lap, waited to see if she'd have any reaction, and placed both hands on the skirt.

"I feel so pink," she said. "Am I pink?"

"No," Danny said, not knowing what she meant. "You're beautiful."

Anne Marie looked up at him. "As in glowing?"

Danny smiled and shook his head. "No, just beautiful." He leaned down and kissed her, then kissed her again, and Anne Marie touched his face.

"Do you smell lemon?" she asked.

He nodded and brushed her hair with the back of his hand.

"Is it me or the dress?"

"You," he said, leaning closer. "And the dress."

Anne Marie looked into his eyes, then remembering Miss Colorado, nudged him so she could get up. "I have to go back," she said, adjusting her toga and clutching the prom dress to her breast. "Will you call me tomorrow?"

"Yes," he said, and walked her across the hall. "Are you all right? It wasn't the dress?"

"I don't know," Anne Marie said. She tapped on Miss Colorado's door. "I don't feel sick anymore, but...." She still felt odd. When the door opened, she stepped inside and glanced back. "Have you ever been to New Orleans, Danny?"

"No, why?" he asked.

"I don't know. I guess I was just wondering."

"Have you?"

"I don't think so."

"Wouldn't you know?"

"I'm not sure."

CHAPTER SIXTEEN

Anne Marie gazed out the bus window as it rumbled past her old building. Today was the day of demolition. An army of men in hard-hats flanked its perimeters. She turned and looked back, remembering, and saw a young woman scaling the wall to the fourth floor, wanting to go back home one more time.

"Listen, Anne," she could hear Jimmie say. "It's not that I don't care about you...."

She stared ahead. At least she'd been able to sleep in her bed last night, and not the tub. And there had been no swishing sounds. Maybe the mouse or rat moved on. And she'd awakened hungry, no nausea. And her mother, according to hospital patient information had had a satisfactory night. And Danny said he'd call. And the dress was at Miss Colorado's, and....

Anne Marie got off the bus at the stop outside Headlands and went to work. It was her anniversary of sorts. She'd been employed here two years today, but didn't expect any fanfare, since she was probably the only one that knew. The rest of the staff had come and gone since then, including the managers. So it was business as usual. She handled the phones, typed resumes, made coffee and appointments, noticed and tried to ignore Jimmie, typed more resumes and cover letters, made more coffee, and in her spare time, made a substantial amount of those dreaded cold calls.

Judy phoned twice in the midst, pleading Phil's case, and then said she'd meet Anne Marie at the hospital to visit her mother. Her mother looked surprised to see them.

"I told you, you didn't have to come."

"That was yesterday," Anne Marie said, as her mother gave Judy a big hug. "I wanted to see how you were doing myself."

"Fine, fine," her mother said. "I told you, it was nothing."

Anne Marie hesitated. If Judy weren't here, she might've brought up what the doctor said. But her mother wouldn't appreciate having, "her dirty laundry being aired," a favorite expression of hers. Or, "crying over spilt milk," which was another. Or, "dwelling on the past." Sometimes her idea of the past came and went in the blink of an eye.

"What a diet," her mother said. "I went to sleep and woke up five pounds thinner. I should sleep for a week."

There'd be nothing left of you then, Anne Marie thought. You'd just be a memory. The past. All in the proverbial blink of an eye.

"What's this I hear about a new boyfriend?" her mother asked, penetrating her reverie.

Anne Marie looked at her. Judy must have told her.

"Well?"

Anne Marie sighed. "He's not exactly a boyfriend. We only went out once."

"And?" Her mother and Judy both looked on expectantly.

"And that's it." She glanced at the urine bag hooked onto the side of the bed. It had streaks of blood at the top and bottom. "How long does the doctor think you'll be here?"

"Oh, not long," her mother said, checking her watch, as if the days were marked off there. "It really was nice of you both to come, but you really don't have to stay."

Dismissed. Anne Marie and Judy said their good-byes and took the elevator downstairs. "Well, that went well," Judy said.

Anne Marie laughed. The two of them had been best friends since grade school, so consequently Judy had been present during all the knock-down, drag-out phases followed by the silent-treatment periods Anne Marie and her mother were basically always going through.

"Let's go get some coffee," Judy said, "and please, please, please, please tell me you found a job for Phil."

There was one, Anne Marie had to admit, and it was perfect for him. A third-shift shopping channel telecommunications operator. Phil liked working nights since he couldn't sleep, and no experience was necessary. She'd run across it in the newspaper while making cold calls today, and in talking with the personnel manager, found out that due to high turnover, they could not afford to be choosy.

That was the clincher. Also, they were looking for someone not averse to flying by the seat of their pants, as the man said. And that too, fit Phil. Not knowing what he was talking about had never stopped him before, so....

Anne Marie took a different bus home and was spared the demolition sight of her old apartment building. Dinner was corn pudding baked in the oven from her grandmother's recipe, and she took Miss Colorado a bowl.

"Why thank you, dear. It's delicious."

Anne Marie thought so too. She especially liked the crusty golden-brown part on top, and she'd given Miss Colorado a generous portion of it. "So how's the dress?" she asked, glancing around for its presence.

"Oh...." Miss Colorado licked her spoon. "It's still here."

Anne Marie laughed. "Anything unusual happen?"

"Yes," Miss Colorado said. "I think I saw it move."

"What?"

Miss Colorado savored another mouthful of pudding. "Actually I think I heard it first. And then I felt a breeze. I can't be sure though, because I was almost asleep."

Anne Marie stiffened with a thought. "Wait a minute. How did it sound when it moved?"

"Well, let me think...." Miss Colorado scraped the bottom of her bowl. "A sort of swishing sound I guess."

Anne Marie nodded, probably the same sound she herself had heard the night before. Back and forth, back and forth. "What am I going to do? What am I going to do?" a voice in her head said. An anguished voice. "What am I going to do?"

"Where is the dress, Miss Colorado?"

"In the bathroom. When I put it in there, the noise stopped."

Hiding, Anne Marie thought. Hiding so no one would hear it, hear her, for hours at a time. "'Tell Laura I love her.' Tell Laura I didn't leave her."

"Excellent pudding, dear."

"I know," Anne Marie said. "Thank you."

Miss Colorado smiled. "Do these types of occurrences happen to you often?"

"The dress you mean, like that? No. Other things, yes. How about you?" Anne Marie asked, already knowing the answer.

"Yes."

"What do you think it means?"

"I don't know," Miss Colorado said. "It might just mean we have very overactive imaginations."

Anne Marie smiled.

"But then again...."

"I think she's trying to tell us something."

Miss Colorado shook her head. "No, dear. I think she's trying to tell you something. In fact I know she's trying to tell you something."

"How? How do you know?"

Miss Colorado hesitated. "The tea leaves."

"You mean there was more?"

"No. Not in yours, dear."

Anne Marie looked at her.

"In mine."

CHAPTER SEVENTEEN

Anne Marie took the dress home. There was no reason why it should keep Miss Colorado awake another night, not in view of what her tea leaves had read. A friend was in need. Not her. A friend.

A friend in need is a friend indeed, she could hear her grandmother reciting, and smiled. Then she thought of what her mother would say, "They all come knocking when they want something," and promptly saddened.

She sighed, hung the dress in her closet, and went to check the cactus. It looked the same, no better, no worse, and dry. Two more days and she could water it again, two more days. She stretched out on the couch and stared at the ceiling. Danny said he'd call and hadn't called yet, unless he phoned while she was across the hall. But then again, wouldn't he call back? She hoped he would. She liked talking to him, liked hearing his voice. She imagined him saying hi in that way of his, and would know from the sound of his voice he'd be smiling, and....

She dozed and woke to a feather of a touch across her cheek. "Who is it?" she asked, fearing an answer.

"Tell Laura I love her. Tell Laura I didn't leave her. Tell Laura not to cry. My love for her will never die."

It's happening, she thought. Jimmie always said I was going to have a nervous breakdown one of these days, that given half a chance I was going to give him one, and now it's happened. I'm having a nervous breakdown.

"Listen," her grandmother's voice said. "Listen."

"I am listening."

"No, you're not. You're talking. I said listen." Her grandmother's voice echoed in her mind. "Listen."

Anne Marie lay perfectly still, and heard the song again.

"'Tell Laura I love her.'"

Again the lightness of a touch on her face.

"Tell Laura I didn't leave her."

"You tell her," Anne Marie said. "What's wrong with you telling her? I don't even know her."

Silence.

"Hello." Anne Marie looked around the room. "Oh that's just great. I pissed 'em off."

"Tell her...."

Anne Marie froze. It was her mother's voice.

"Tell her."

She lay listening and listening, until the phone rang, and jumped up to answer it before it rang again. Danny, it would be Danny. And sanity.

It was the hospital. "Miss Light?"

"Yes."

"Your mother didn't want you notified, but as her next of kin...."

Anne Marie stared.

"As you know, your mother has a "Do Not Resuscitate' clause in her living will."

Anne Marie shook her head no, she didn't know.

"Which states no heroic measures in the event of cardiac arrest."

Anne Marie sat down on the edge of the tub. "Is she...?"

"Oh no, no, she's fine, and didn't want us to phone you, by the way. But we felt you would want to know. Her heart has stopped briefly twice tonight. Both times it has started back up on its own, however...."

"I'll be right down."

"No, please. She's sleeping now and insisted on our not alarming you. She's says she's fine and that you have work in the morning, and that she didn't want you down here just to watch her sleep."

Anne Marie shook her head and smiled. She could hear her mother saying that, hear the precise tone of her voice, the practicality. She thanked the nurse for phoning her, thanked her twice actually, said she'd come visit her mother tomorrow, and hung up the phone.

She wondered what she would do if her mother died, wondered if she'd find herself wishing there was something she should have said, wondered if....

She fell asleep a little after midnight, but woke repeatedly to a sense that someone was there watching her, waiting, hovering, intruding, and ended up covering her head with her pillow. That didn't help, though. The feeling only got stronger.

"Enough," she finally said. "Enough."

She got out of bed, put on her robe and slippers, yanked the dress out of her closet, and stormed out of her apartment. She had just a bit too much going on in her own life at the moment as far as she was concerned, to make room for this. And why hadn't Danny called?

The first trashcan was full, the second overflowing. She headed for the third, and gasped when she heard a noise behind her.

"Hey," her veteran neighbor said. "How's it going?"

She clutched the dress to her chest, trying to catch her breath, and wondered. What on earth was he doing sitting on his window ledge, and at this hour of the morning? "Okay. How about you?"

He shrugged and glanced at the dress, then smiled. "You want some coffee?"

Anne Marie hesitated. "Sure."

He looked at her. "You got a cup?"

She smiled; he had a sense of humor. "No."

"Hold on." He leaned back, balancing himself on the window ledge as he reached for one, and Anne Marie found herself smiling again. He looked a little like Humpty Dumpty, teetering back and forth. "You don't take sugar, do you?" he asked.

"No, black's fine."

"What? You don't like cream?"

She smiled again; she was literally talking to his bare feet. "No, I like cream."

"Okay." When he sat up straight he had two cups, one for her and another fresh one for him and lots of cream in both. "Bottoms up," he said.

Anne Marie thanked him and took a sip, as hot as it was delicious.

"I grind my own grounds," he told her, to which she nodded her appreciation. And they both heard a screeching sound above them then, a screen being raised.

"Do you two want to keep it down? Some of us are sleeping, you know."

Anne Marie laughed; she couldn't help herself. Their voices had barely been above a whisper, and compared to the noise this man normally made.... "Sorry," she said, and strained to see who it was. The lesbian. Miss Congeniality.

The woman leaned out. "What's with the dress?"

Anne Marie looked at it; having forgotten it was still tucked under her arm.

"What dress?" another voice said, her companion's, as she wedged herself through the window beside her. "Where?"

The veteran shook his head.

"Oh, how pretty."

"Shhhhh...."

No one seemed to know where that came from.

"Sorry," Anne Marie said, to whoever it was. After all, this whole thing started with her. The nice lesbian waved and the two disappeared then, the screen screeching again as it was lowered back down, and the veteran shrugged.

Anne Marie finished her coffee, thanked him in a whisper as she handed over the cup, and started back inside only to come face to face with the Super.

He smiled. "Well, aren't you up early."

Anne Marie nodded. There didn't seem to be much to say. "What time is it anyway?"

"Five-ten," he said, glancing at his watch. "Everything all right with your apartment?"

"Fine," she said, and wondered what he'd say if she told him it had been the dress making her sick, and that now for some reason it wasn't. "Thanks for your help."

He waved and walked on, as if he had something very important to do, and Anne Marie went back into her apartment, laid the dress on the living room chair, and sat down and stared at it.

"All right," she said, with a resigned sigh of reluctance. "What is it exactly you want me to do? Who's Laura? And how do I go about telling her what you want her to know?"

CHAPTER EIGHTEEN

Anne Marie couldn't believe her eyes. She'd expected to see at least a few remains of her old building. A stone, a brick, a rusty steel beam or two. But there was nothing. It had been rendered to a vacant lot.

She thought about old Mr. Murphy on the second floor, how he used to grow beefsteak tomatoes on his balcony and how juicy they were. How proud he used to be. "I'm not going to no goddamn nursing home," he'd said. And yet that's precisely where he'd ended up.

Jimmie had a note waiting for her on her desk when she arrived at work. She sat down, holding her breath. "It's urgent," the message read. "I need to talk to you."

"Oh, Lord."

"Did you hear?" a co-worker asked, having appeared at her side. "Jimmie's getting married."

Anne Marie stared.

"Anne Marie? Anne Marie, did you hear me?"

She nodded, and then nodded again. "Yes. Yes, of course I did," she said, and wondered where the ladies room was, wondered how she could work here two years and all of sudden forget its location. She looked around.

When the phone rang, she willed herself to answer it, feeling numb. "Good morning, Headlands Ink," she said, clutching the receiver.

It was Judy. She'd lost the address for Phil's interview. "I can't find it anywhere. Can you give it to me again?"

Anne Marie searched through the job file, relayed the information, and Judy thanked her. "I'll talk to you later."

"Wait," Anne Marie said, and had to clear her throat. "Jimmie's getting married."

"What? That prick!"

Anne Marie looked up and watched her co-worker walk away, realizing only then she'd been standing there all this time. "Cherise told me. She's new and didn't know."

Judy sighed sympathetically. "Are you all right?"

"Yes, I'm fine," Anne Marie said. If she could only feel her arms and legs again.

Judy tried to cheer her up. "Come on, he's history. You don't need him anymore. You have your telephone man now."

"No, I don't. He didn't call."

Silence. Judy didn't know how to respond. "Maybe he was working."

"Right," Anne Marie said. "And he couldn't find a phone anywhere."

Judy laughed in spite of herself. "Come on, he'll call. He sounded really nice."

He is nice, Anne Marie thought, too nice for me, a woman who talks to dresses and doesn't know if she's coming or going. "Tell Phil good luck."

Judy paused. "Are you serious?"

"Yes."

"Oh, God...you are depressed."

Anne Marie laughed halfheartedly. "No, I'm not. I'm fine. Honest. I'll talk to you later." She hung up and stared at Jimmie's note, then threw it away, and thanks to the busy phones, kept occupied until noon. She never asked for favors, but needed one today, and asked her boss if she could have an extra half-hour for lunch so she could visit her mother.

She wanted to talk to the doctor and thought if she waited until evening, he probably wouldn't be available then. Her boss told her no problem; she took the bus to save time, and rode up in the elevator with four nurses toting lunch trays from the cafeteria.

Anne Marie's stomach growled. Her mother hadn't eaten yet either. She said she was a little under the weather, an expression she used to use often that always baffled Anne Marie. Under the weather. What if it was sunny?

Anne Marie sat down next to the bed. Her mother looked weary. But then again, how was a person who literally died twice in the same night supposed to look? Happy, happy to be alive. Under sunny skies. Anne Marie glanced out the window; it was cloudy.

"Do you want me to go get you some cottage cheese?" Her mother ate cottage cheese daily, no matter what. And not the good kind, with all the creamy milk fat, the dietetic stuff. The kind with those icky little curds Anne Marie remembered counting all over her plate as a rebellious teen to the sum of fifty-nine and sixty-four and sometimes even more amazing, sixty or seventy right on the dot per serving. "I'm sure they have some in the cafeteria."

"No," her mother said. "But thank you."

Anne Marie nodded. She didn't have much time. "Mom, I talked to your doctor."

"You did? Why? I told you it was nothing."

"I know. But that's not what he says."

Her mother narrowed her eyes and stiffened visibly. "Don't you have to get back to work?"

Anne Marie glanced at the clock on the wall. "Yes, but I thought...."

"Don't go looking for trouble, Anne Marie. It'll find you soon enough."

Anne Marie shook her head. "What, you mean me in particular...or you? Or are we talking about the whole world in general?" Now wasn't exactly the time to pick a fight, but just once, she wished her mother would respond genuinely and not according to someone else's rules. Just once. "Please...."

"I'm tired, Anne Marie," her mother said instead, and in that dismissive way of hers. "I'm tired, and...."

"In pain," Anne Marie said. "I can see that."

Her mother looked at her, just looked at her for a moment, then turned and stared out the window. Anne Marie was in pain as well. "All right. What did the doctor say?"

"He said you may have to undergo chemotherapy."

"I told them no."

"I know. But he thinks in time, you'll change your mind, and I...."

"Anne Marie, enough of this. Look at what you see and not what you think you see, for once. All right?"

Anne Marie stood up to leave; this was an old argument, the auras.

"Wait!" her mother said.

Anne Marie stopped at the door, watched her mother open her mouth to say something else, watched her hesitate, and watched her change her mind. It was the closest they'd ever come as far as Anne Marie was concerned, to being a real mother and daughter, ever. But the moment came and went, just like that.

"I'll see you tomorrow," Anne Marie said.

"You don't have to come."

"I know."

Headlands Ink was a madhouse when she returned. "When there's hay to be made, you make hay," her boss kept saying, as he paced back and forth cheering the hands on. "Lift that bale." She wondered if he was somehow related to her mother. On the bus ride home, she dozed with her head against the window, and got a stiff neck. She'd been able to avoid Jimmie all day, but what about tomorrow? And why had he come to her apartment? Twice yet. What could he possibly have had to say? Did he want to break the news to her himself? To spare her?

She filled her tub with hot water, as hot as she could stand, stripped, and immersed herself to her chin. He loves you, he loves you not. He loves you, he loves you not.

The phone rang. "Hello," she said, the water drip dripping from her arm.

It was Judy. "Phil got the job, he starts tomorrow night! He's so excited. He says this job was made for him."

"Good. I'm glad."

"We're going out to celebrate. He told me to call and see if you want to come along."

"No, thanks but...."

"Come on."

Anne Marie stared at the water on the floor. "You two go on. I'll talk to you tomorrow."

She hung up the phone and thought about Danny, thought about his smile, and sank back into the water. This had not been a good day, far too much to deal with. She'd talked to a dress that had her attention now, but refused to speak. Danny hadn't called. Jimmie was getting married. And her mother was going to die.

"Count your blessings," she could hear her grandmother say.

"What blessings?" She closed her eyes and waited, listened, but even her grandmother refused to speak now, and she'd never felt so alone. She heard a noise outside her apartment then, a loud noise, then shouting.

"Medic, medic! Medic, medic!!

"Medic, medic! Medic, medic!!"

This was followed by loud pounding on her door.

Pounding on the next door.

And the next.

And the next.

"Oh, dear God..." she said, shivering in the water.

"It's Kiwalski, Sir! I think he's dead!

"He's dead, Sir!

"Medic, medic! Medic, medic!!"

CHAPTER NINETEEN

Anne Marie sat bolt upright from a troubled sleep and panicked when a ray of sunshine nearly blinded her. "Oh no!" She'd slept in. "Damn it!"

She hurried into the bathroom, practically peed on the run, brushed her teeth and washed her face, raked a comb through her hair, and ran into the bedroom and dressed in a flurry. If she were lucky, if the buses ran on time, if every light was green, and....

No such luck. She arrived at work ten minutes after nine, the very first time in two years she'd ever been late. And it did not go unnoticed. Everyone looked at her as if she were a stranger in their midst.

"Miss Light," her boss said, scowling. "Can I see you in my office a moment."

She trailed behind him like a puppy. "I'm so sorry. I have no excuse aside from the fact that I slept in, and...."

"Have a seat," he said, and closed the door.

Anne Marie sat down.

"I'm disappointed in you, Anne Marie," the man said, hands in his pockets and walking around his desk to face her.

Anne Marie looked at him. She'd already said she was sorry, what did he want? Blood? She'd never ever been late before. In two years. Two whole years.

"Very, very disappointed," he said.

Anne Marie stared.

"It's one thing to behave carelessly, I can maybe forgive that. But to...."

Anne Marie watched his color change, and didn't like the red glow.

The man sat down and picked up a piece of paper, a job listing. "Even though you are only a receptionist, the fact that you have privy to the various positions...."

Only a receptionist? Anne Marie continued staring, first at the paper in his hand, then his face again. The color red could be so ugly at times. And no good could come of it.

"I see a trend," he said. "And I've been warned."

"Warned of what?"

"Your irresponsibility," the man said.

"My irresponsibility?" Anne Marie couldn't believe this. "What irresponsibility?"

Her boss waved the job listing like a fan. "I've been informed that not only do you answer the phone in a less than professional manner...."

Anne Marie shook her head. What was he talking about? And what did this have to do with her being late?

"We are not Headlands Ink."

Anne Marie looked at him.

"That is not how we answer the phone."

"Wait a minute. Are you saying I...?"

"Precisely, and it was overheard. The person does not want to be identified, but takes pride in her, I mean, their work, and brought it to my attention only because...."

Cherise. It had to be Cherise, Anne Marie thought. But why?

"I've also been told you are supplying Headlands Employment Agency job listings to certain people not under contract, and that just yesterday, one of those people secured a position over one of ours, which resulted in a lost fee, and...."

Phil? How on earth?

"I didn't want to believe it at first, but in talking with some others in our organization...."

Anne Marie zoned out, the rest of what he said falling on deaf ears. "Well?" she finally heard him say.

"Uh. Well, what?"

He frowned. "What do you have to say for yourself?"

She said the first thing that came to her mind. "I don't think it's right to charge a fee for jobs advertised in the paper."

"I see," the man said, rocking in his chair, his red glow blending into what her grandmother always dubbed a perfect shade of shit brown. "I see."

Anne Marie glanced out the window, where perched on the sill, sat a raven. Death.

"I have no alternative but to let you go," her boss said.

"What?" Anne Marie looked at him.

"You're terminated."

Anne Marie saw her finances flash before her eyes. "I don't understand. You're firing me because I gave out an address that was in the newspaper and supposedly answered the phone one time saying...?"

The man held up his hand. "I see a trend, and for the good of the company...."

"What trend?" Anne Marie rose indignantly.

"Yesterday you needed time off, today you're late. What's it going to be tomorrow?"

"Nothing. My mother's in the hospital. You told me there was no problem taking the time yesterday. And I've only been late this one time. Why are you doing this?"

The man shook his head and heaved a sigh. "I've taken the liberty to check with your past employer."

"What?"

"He says you were notoriously late, and irresponsible."

"That was years ago. I don't see what...."

The man stood as well now. "I'm sorry, Anne Marie. But as I said, for the good of the company...."

Anne Marie swallowed hard. "As of when?" she asked, accepting her fate.

"As of now. I'll accompany you as you clean out your desk."

"Accompany me?"

He motioned to the door. "And please, do not cause a scene. We have clients in the office."

CHAPTER TWENTY

Anne Marie stared at the cactus. She'd thought of going to the hospital on her way home, but her mother would only want to know why she wasn't at work, would probably assume she'd talked to the doctor again and had gotten even grimmer news, and…. She'd have to go later in the day, she decided, even though it would mean another bus fare. She had no choice.

She imagined her mother telling her not to waste her money, all the more reason to go. She imagined her mother realizing she cared then. She imagined this all being a dream.

Fired? Me?

"This can't be real. It can't be."

It occurred to her that she should eat something and that she should go buy a newspaper to search the want ads, but her aches and pains were back, particularly in her left shoulder and arm. She wondered how long she had on her hospitalization, weeks, a month? Or if they, like her employer, could and would just cut her off. She wondered if she had a serious disease. She wondered if she too was dying.

A soft knock on the door startled her. Probably the raven, she told herself. And it did sound a little like pecking. She pictured it pacing out in the hall, back and forth, turning its little head, ruffling its black and blue feathers.

"Anne Marie? Anne Marie?"

She recognized Miss Colorado's tiny voice.

"Anne Marie? Anne Marie, are you home?"

She opened the door and stared. Miss Colorado was dressed in black from head to toe, spider veil draped over her eyes and all. "Wow!" Anne Marie said. "Who died?"

"Anton," Miss Colorado said. "Eight years ago today. Why are you home? Are you ill?"

"No." Anne Marie invited her in but she declined. "I got fired."

"Oh my. Why?"

"Well." Anne Marie drew a breath and sighed. "I've been giving that a lot of thought."

"And?"

"I still don't know. It's like I'm cursed or something."

Miss Colorado nodded, said there were times in her life she'd felt the same way, and turned to leave but then stopped. "Did you hear him last night?" she asked, remembering.

"Yes," Anne Marie said, glancing at the veteran's door. "I feel so sorry for him."

"Me too. He can't forget."

Anne Marie nodded. "Miss Colorado?"

"Yes, dear?"

"How did Anton die?"

Miss Colorado hesitated. "His heart gave out. It was enlarged, they said, twice the size of a normal man's. But I already knew that."

"How?"

"How?" Miss Colorado smiled a sad smile. "For one, he wasn't a normal man. He was different. I knew it. The people knew it. The lions knew it. I think it was because he had so much heart."

Anne Marie studied what she could see of her expression under the web of her black veil. "Were you with him when he died?"

Miss Colorado nodded. He'd died in her arms. "He was in the cage with his lions, and the lions wouldn't let anyone enter but me." Her voice cracked, her tiny shoulders trembling as she disappeared behind her door, and in time, alone, Anne Marie retreated as well.

She wished she had a CD, so she could put on the headphones and turn it up real loud and lose herself in the beat. Drums, she wanted to hear drums, hard and fast, to drown out the sound of her pulse, the throbbing, the ringing in her ears.

It was the phone, which took a moment to realize, and she ran to answer it. "Hello."

Silence.

"Hello."

Nothing. Anne Marie hung up. "Well, if you don't want to talk to me, the hell with you. I don't want to talk to you either. I have enough problems."

She washed her face, and because it still felt dirty, washed it again. "Get back in there right now, young lady," she could hear her mother say, "and do it right this time. Use soap."

"I did use soap."

"Go!"

She looked in the mirror, saw her face get cloudy then pink all over, and waited for her eyes to focus. What you have to do, she told herself, is pay the rent. It wasn't due for another two weeks, but if she paid it now, regardless of what else might happen, she reasoned, she wouldn't be put out on the street. She went to get her checkbook, balanced to the penny always, wrote a check, and made herself a sandwich.

The phone rang again, and this time it was her mother. "What happened at work?" she asked. "I called and they said you were no longer employed there. What did you do?"

Anne Marie stared at the tub. Her mother never phoned her at work. Why today? Grandmother, she thought, help me. Help me know what to say.

"Anne Marie?"

"I'm thinking."

Her mother sighed. "Well anyway, the reason I called you. I need a copy of my will. Do you still have keys to the house?"

"I don't know. I'll have to look." She searched through her belongings in her mind. If they were anywhere, they'd be in her jewelry box.

"Let me know if you don't have them. I have a set here, but I don't want you to have to come all the way down to the hospital just to get them."

"Why do you need your will?"

"I want to double check something."

"Couldn't you just call your attorney?"

"I tried. He's out of town and won't be back until next week. That'll be too late."

"Too late for what?"

Her mother sighed. "Oh, Anne Marie please, do we have to do this?"

"Do what?" Anne Marie used to always say, though refraining now. "I'll stop by on the way."

Since she had all afternoon she decided she might as well walk, and set out. Though her mother's house was worlds away theoretically, in actual distance it was less than two miles. And oddly enough, given her circumstances of the day, she felt good walking, almost carefree. The closer she got however, the more worrisome she became. She couldn't remember the last time she'd been in the house alone. It had to be before she ran away. That long. She didn't even know any of the neighbors anymore. They'd all gone South.

She wondered if she should check the mail, decided not to, and climbed the steps to the front door.

"Yoo hoo! Oh you there, Miss!"

Anne Marie turned.

"There's no one home," a middle-aged woman two doors down said.

"I know. I'm Rebecca's daughter," Anne Marie explained, thinking that would be enough.

"Really? Rebecca never said anything about having a daughter."

Anne Marie took the house key out of her pocket, waved it for further substantiation, opened the screen and unlocked the door. The living room lights were on. The living room lights were always on. "It makes people think you're home," her mother used to say.

"Well, now that we are home, can we turn them off?"

"No, then people'll think...."

Anne Marie looked around. Her mother said the copy of the will would either be in the top desk drawer or in the cubbyhole in the kitchen over the spice rack. It turned out to be in the cubbyhole, along with her father's pouch of foreign currency from the war. Anne Marie wondered why her mother kept it after all these years; the currency was worthless. She remembered hearing her father say it himself.

"Which is why he left it behind," her mother told her, when Anne Marie was but ten years old. "Believe you me, if it was worth anything...."

Anne Marie tucked her mother's will into her back pocket, locked the front door as she left, and turned into the flash of a camera.

"I'll have your picture if you took anything," the neighbor lady said, standing at a safe distance and adjusting the lens to snap another.

Anne Marie posed; arms crossed and with a defiant look so her mother would be sure to recognize her, and then laughed.

"I'm sorry," she said. "Honest, I'm a daughter. My mom's in the hospital and wanted me to stop by for something."

The woman looked at her warily. "How's she doing?"

"Okay. She should be home in a couple of days."

"Tell her Sophie said hi."

"I'll do that." Anne Marie walked to the bus stop, stood for a few minutes waiting, and decided she might as well just keep right on walking. The hospital was probably a good five miles, but why not.

Her mother was just finishing her dinner when she finally arrived, and looked up from her tray with expectation. "Did you get it?"

Anne Marie nodded.

"Good." Her mother immediately rang for the nurse. "All we need now is a witness."

Anne Marie eased herself into a chair. This urgency was nothing new; everything always had to be done right now with her. She never gave it a thought, and consequently was anything but prepared when her mother scribbled something, had the nurse witness it, and sat back with an announcement.

"There," Rebecca Light said, folding her hands over her still-tender incision and closing her eyes. "Now I can die in peace."

CHAPTER TWENTY-ONE

Anne Marie dropped her rent check off with the Super, thanked him when he said he'd give it to his wife who did the books, and entered her apartment feeling relieved that at least that much was done.

She'd stopped for a newspaper on the way home from the hospital, planned to spend the evening combing the want ads, and went through the motions. She made a small pot of coffee, ate scrambled eggs and toast, changed into a pair of sweat pants and a T-shirt, and sat down next to the cactus to begin.

"Wait a minute." The plant was changing color, turning yellowish. "Were you like this this morning?" she asked, thinking if it were, she surely would've noticed. "What's this mean?" In a person, turning yellow wouldn't be good. In fact, when it came right down to it, yellow was Anne Marie's least favorite color. She associated it with liver problems and with death, ever since Grandmother Light....

The phone rang, and it was Judy, raving about how much Phil loved his job. "He says it's great!"

Anne Marie smiled. At least something was going good for somebody, even if it had to be Phil.

"Did your telephone man call?"

"No."

"I'm sorry."

"Yeah, me too I guess."

"Why? What do you mean you guess? I thought you said he was nice."

"He is nice," Anne Marie said, and changed the subject. "My mom says she's dying."

"Oh my God. Is she?"

"I don't know. She may have to have chemotherapy, depending on her biopsy. She changed her will."

"To what?"

"I don't know. I don't want to know. I sealed the envelope."

"You amaze me."

Anne Marie shrugged. Me, amazing? No. She found herself reciting Miss Colorado. "The amazing, the death defying...."

Judy laughed. "Do you want to do something?"

"No." Anne Marie glanced into the living room at the classifieds spread all over the couch. "It's too late, besides I'm tired. I walked to my mom's and then the hospital."

"What? Why?"

"I don't know. I guess I just felt like it."

"Your legs are probably killing you."

Anne Marie shifted her weight back and forth. "Actually, they don't feel that bad." Which was weird, she thought, and figured she'd pay tomorrow. "Did you hear about Headlands?"

"No, why? What happened?"

Anne Marie hesitated. If she hadn't heard, then there was no reason why she should know all the particulars. She'd just feel bad then. "I don't work there anymore."

"What? As of when?"

"As of this morning. I cleared myself out and I'm gone."

Judy didn't understand. "Because of Jimmie?"

"Yeah, probably, that and other things. My boss got on me about being late and taking off yesterday to see my mom."

"What an asshole."

Anne Marie chuckled.

"Did you find another job yet?"

"No, I'm looking now."

"Don't worry, you'll find one. Do you remember any from work?"

Anne Marie hesitated again, a sore spot. "No, I've been too preoccupied lately to pay attention."

"Well, at least you won't have to see Jimmie every day now."

Anne Marie stared. She hadn't really thought of that. "He's been coming over here."

"What? Why? What does he want?"

"I don't know, I'm never home."

"Good God!"

Anne Marie laughed, more for Judy's sake than her own, and again changed the subject. "Do you remember that oatmeal bread my grandmother used to make?"

"Yeah, with the raisins?"

"I think I'm going to make some." She ran through a mental list of the ingredients. All she'd need to buy were the raisins. "I'll make you one too, I'll let you know."

When they hung up, Anne Marie went back to see if there was any change in the cactus, hoping that it had been her imagination. But sure enough, it was yellowing. She thought about phoning the man at the nursery again, but didn't really like his attitude, and looked up another greenhouse instead.

"I'd almost have to see it to say for sure," this particular horticulturist said. "Can you bring it in?"

"Well, it is kinda heavy, but I guess I could try. What are your hours tomorrow?"

"Nine to seven," the man said.

Anne Marie had no idea how she could get it there, obviously lugging it twenty some blocks was out of the question.

"Ask for Milt."

"Okay, but it's due to be watered tomorrow. Should I water it before I come?"

"No, let me take a look at it first."

Anne Marie circled several ads in the paper, numbered them in order of preference, and showered and got ready for bed. The best thing to do with days like this, her grandmother used to say, was to put them behind you.

"That's right," her mother would always add. "Tomorrow just might be worse."

Anne Marie hoped not, and relived the scene at Headlands this morning; her boss standing there, apparently to make sure she didn't take anything that wasn't hers, and the way everyone kept looking at her, how the phone rang and was answered right in front of her, how she refused to look in Jimmie's direction....

She shuddered and thought about what her mother would say if she knew the circumstances of what had happened at work. She thought about her mother dying. She thought about her mother living. She thought about her grandmother's mirrors the day of her funeral, and how she kept looking for her face and almost didn't recognize it because it looked so much like her own. She thought about Anton and his lions and his widow draped in black. She thought about a frightened pregnant girl in a pink prom dress. She thought about war, and about New Orleans. And ultimately, just before she fell asleep, she thought about Danny. Miss Colorado must've been wrong. He wasn't the one. He couldn't be. If he was, he would've called.

CHAPTER TWENTY-TWO

Anne Marie scanned the back alley for an abandoned shopping cart, remembered seeing one on her way to the supermarket the other day, and set out on foot.

"Hey, where're you going?" her veteran neighbor shouted from his window. "Where's the fire?"

Anne Marie waved. "Nowhere, I have to find a shopping cart."

"Oh yeah? What size?"

Anne Marie laughed. What size? "Oh, medium I guess."

"Sorry, can't help you then."

Anne Marie played along. "But any size'll do."

"Then you're in luck," he said, motioning he'd just be a minute. "One shopping cart coming right up."

Anne Marie waited, watched, and listened. And out he came, grinning and trailing a jumbo cart behind him. "I've been meaning to return it anyway."

Anne Marie looked at him.

"One of my buddies pushed me home in it one night. It doesn't have a name on it."

Anne Marie smiled. "It's nice to have friends," she said, and the veteran nodded and laughed.

"If someone asks...."

"I'll tell them I found it. Thanks." Anne Marie retrieved the cactus, heaved it up and over the side of the cart, and headed for the nursery.

The horticulturist was a man of few words. "Hmmm," he kept saying, as he circled the plant still in the cart. "Hmmm." When he reached in to lift it out, Anne Marie all but threw herself between them.

"Don't do anything without telling me what you're going to do first."

"I wouldn't think of it."

"Good." Anne Marie stepped aside warily. "It's been hurt enough as it is."

The man raised the plant, and with the utmost care, placed it on his worktable. "Well, the way I see it you have two choices."

Anne Marie studied his face.

"Cut it off right here." He motioned to just below where the bend had been. "I can do it for you if you like."

"Or...?"

He circled the plant again. "Or, you leave it as it is and see what happens."

Anne Marie liked that option better. Just as long as, "What'll happen if...?"

"If you leave it?"

She nodded.

The man frowned. "I'm not sure. As a species, this is a hardy plant. But I have to be honest, I don't like the looks of this one."

Anne Marie had to agree. "It's yellow, isn't it?"

"Yes. And that's strange."

"Maybe it just needs water."

The man shook his head. "I don't think so. The soil's not completely dry, and look here...." He pointed out how supple the cactus was, pressed a side of it gently between his fingers, and shook his head. "I think if anything, it's in shock."

"What?"

"In shock. How long has it been since this happened?"

"I don't know, a week, almost two. Do you think it's been in shock all that time?"

"Could be. Would you like to leave it here for a few days so I can keep an eye on it?"

"No, I'd rather take it home. It's used to being with me."

The man nodded and smiled, as if he figured as much, and for a moment, a very somber moment, the two of them stood commiserating with the cactus. It was as yellow as can be.

"But in the event...."

Anne Marie froze. "Use a sharp knife," she could hear him say, his voice sounding as if he were at the end of a tunnel. "Cut it right here...." Just the thought of it made her nauseous, the room suddenly swaying, and she gripped the shopping cart. "And let the top dry for a day or two, and then plant it."

"What?"

"The top. Let it dry out for twenty-four hours or so, and plant it."

"You mean the bottom is what'll die?"

"No, not necessarily. If all goes well, it'll heal and sprout new shoots."

Anne Marie smiled a relieved smile, but all too soon it vanished, because he went on to explain how there was no rhyme or reason to these things, how both top and bottom could very well die, particularly since this yellowing was such a puzzle, and how sometimes even if you do everything right, take all the necessary precautions, and....

As Anne Marie rounded the corner of the last block to home, she heard someone call her name, and turned. It was Danny.

He looked at her oddly. "Anne Marie?"

She nodded. Who else?

He put something in his truck and walked toward her. "What are you doing?"

She glanced away. What business was it of his? "I had to take the plant to the nursery. It's in shock."

Danny looked at the cactus, went to touch it for some reason, and Anne Marie grabbed his hand. "Don't!" she said, and turned on her heels. "Nice seeing you."

"Wait!"

She stopped and stared at him, waited, waited, and waited, but all he did was stand there, apparently with nothing to say, so she turned again.

"I don't know about you, Anne Marie."

"What?"

He smiled hesitantly, and glanced around. "Can I come over later?"

"Why?"

He shrugged. "I don't know. To talk."

Anne Marie looked at him. You're not the one. You're not the one. If you were the one...? "What time?"

"You name it."

"Fine, eight," she said, thinking what a fool she was. What if he doesn't come? After all, he said he'd call before and didn't. What if he doesn't show? You don't need another Jimmie. You don't need more lies. You don't need anyone.

Danny smiled again, that smile from the first day they met, and Anne Marie shook her head. "Listen," she said. "Unless you have a good reason for not calling when you said you would, don't bother, okay?"

"Okay," he said. "I'll see you at eight."

CHAPTER TWENTY-THREE

Miss Colorado seemed quite worried. "Where have you been, dear?"

"Everywhere." Anne Marie eased her tired body into the chair. "I first took the cactus to the nursery, then I went to the supermarket around the corner to return the cart, but it wasn't theirs. They said it looked like one of the ones from Fazio's and gave me directions, but it didn't belong to them either."

"What cart?"

"The veteran's. He gave it to me for the cactus and I told him I'd return it to wherever it came from, only...."

Miss Colorado nodded, remembering the night the young man slept in the hall stuffed inside it, legs and arms dangling, and how in the morning, apparently confused, he tipped it over with a crash and a bang and fought his way out.

"Anyway." Anne Marie had ended up going to five different supermarkets before finally finding the right one, bought a box of raisins, and since she was close to the hospital, walked from there to visit her mother.

"How is she doing?"

"Okay. She starts chemotherapy tomorrow. If all goes well, they're going to send her home Monday."

Miss Colorado nodded thoughtfully. "Is she a tea drinker?"

"Yes, why?"

"I'll mix her up something to settle her stomach."

"Thank you." Anne Marie smiled. "Well, I'd better get going. Danny's supposed to come over."

"The telephone man?"

"Yes." Anne Marie stood up to leave, but hesitated. "Miss Colorado, you said he was the one. The one what?"

Miss Colorado shrugged her tiny shoulders. "You'll know."

"When?"

"When it's time."

Danny arrived right at eight with a bouquet of white carnations, which he presented first, then one long-stemmed red rose, still in the bud stage, and after that, a bottle of wine. "Actually, it's grape juice," he said, pointing out the label. "I thought wine might be overdoing it."

Anne Marie smiled. "I think so too, I don't have any wine glasses. But now juice glasses...."

Danny sat down on the couch in the living room and watched as Anne Marie put the flowers in a fish bowl. "I'm sorry," she said. "I don't have a vase either. I used to, I think, but I'm not sure." Jimmie was never big on flowers, though he did buy her more than one goldfish.

"So...." She placed the flowers in the bowl on the end table, and sat down on the opposite corner of the couch. "Since you're here." Maybe if Miss Colorado hadn't insisted he was the one, it wouldn't matter that he hadn't called, and maybe she wouldn't have given him another thought. Maybe if....

"It's you, Anne Marie. I don't know how to take you."

"What? What do you mean?"

"I mean the way you are."

"And that's why you didn't call?"

Danny paused and then nodded.

"Because of the way I am?"

"Come on, Anne Marie, you fainted on me our first night. And you got this thing with the cactus and that dress. You're weird."

"Thank you. Shall we have our grape juice now?"

Danny laughed. "I'm serious. You scare me and yet...." He fell silent and swallowed hard. "I'm sorry. I should've called. I just didn't know what to say."

Anne Marie looked at him and sighed. Leave it to me, she thought, if this is the one. He thinks I'm weird already, and he hasn't even seen the half of it. Wait till I'm having a really good day.

"Hush," she heard her grandmother say. "Hush and let the man talk."

"But what if he lies?"

"Hush. What if he tells the truth?"

"Anne Marie?"

She looked at him.

"It's just that I've never met anyone like you before. When I'm with you and you do all these weird things...."

Anne Marie stared. Maybe this *was* the truth.

"The only thing I can think about is, so what, I want to be with you so it doesn't matter. But then when I'm somewhere else and I think about some of the things you do...."

Anne Marie nodded. He needn't say any more. He should just leave. She would if she were him.

"And then when I stopped by the other day and that guy was here."

"What guy?"

"I don't know. I didn't ask. He was sitting outside your apartment."

Jimmie. She shook her head. Him again. "Will you excuse me," she said.

Danny nodded.

Anne Marie went into the bathroom and locked the door. If only her mind didn't work the way it did. As it was, she'd just remembered about that pair of underwear of hers stashed on top of the medicine cabinet, a continuation of her weirdness should Danny happen to have to come in here. She looked around for a place to hide them, and ended up stuffing them into an old decorator soap dish shaped like a tulip, and laughed to herself. It was then the phone rang, and she jumped a mile.

"Jesus!" She grabbed for it and said hello.

"Anne Marie?"

"Yes."

"'Tell Laura I love her.'"

"What?"

"Tell Laura I didn't leave her."

"Who is this?" It was a woman's voice.

"Tell Laura not to cry."

"No."

"My love for her will never die."

Anne Marie hung up the phone, reconsidered, and picked it right back up, but by then it was a just a dial tone.

"Danny! Danny, come here quick." She opened the door. "Can you tell me who just called?"

"I can try," he said, looking at her oddly again. "Why? Was it a prank?"

"I don't know." She started trembling, all color draining from her face. "It's this message I keep hearing in my head. Did you hear the phone ring?"

"Yes." He took the receiver from her and dialed star sixty-nine.

"I'm sorry," a recorded operator said. "This service cannot be...."

"Bullshit!" Danny pressed the dial and punched in another succession of numbers. "Did you block the service?" he asked Anne Marie.

She shook her head no. How could she block a service?

"Yeah, this is Danny. Give me the last callback on 555-2616."

Anne Marie sat down on the edge of the tub and stared at the floor.

"What do you mean? It couldn't have been more'n three or four minutes ago," Danny insisted. "It just rang! Try it again."

Anne Marie picked at a scratch on her arm. If she could only get all the skin off.

"Don't!" Danny said, and turned her chin up so she'd look at him. "What did they say?"

She shook her head. "You don't want to know."

"Yes I do." He motioned for her to wait while he finished talking with the operator. "All right, thanks. But make sure it's on after this, okay?" He hung up quickly and asked again, "Now what did they say?"

Anne Marie withdrew deep into herself, and didn't know whether she should tell him or not? "No," she could imagine her mother saying. "He'll think you're crazy for sure and you'll never see him again. It'll be adios, you hear me, mark my words."

"Anne Marie?" Danny knelt down on one knee in front of her. "If you're being harassed, we'll file a report. Come on, now tell me. Is it that guy from out in the hall?"

"No." She shook her head. Why would he suspect Jimmie? "It was a woman."

"Someone you know?"

She shrugged. "I'm not sure."

"What do you mean?"

"I'm mean, I'm not sure. I think somehow..." She hesitated and shuddered, remembering the tone of voice. "I think somehow, the woman was me."

"What?"

"I think it was me." Tears welled up in her eyes. "It was me, Danny. I think it was me."

CHAPTER TWENTY-FOUR

Danny didn't understand. But for that matter, neither did Anne Marie. "I'm sorry. Maybe you should just go now," she said to spare both of them.

"No, I'm not going anywhere." He took her gently by the hand, led her back into the living room, and sat down next to her on the couch. "Now tell me again."

Anne Marie wiped her eyes and drew a deep breath and sighed. "The phone rang and at first I didn't recognize the voice, but then I did. It was mine."

Danny shook his head and looked away in frustration.

"You're wishing you'd never met me, aren't you?" Anne Marie said.

"No." He smiled. "Actually I was wishing I'd moved the phone out here, that way I could've...."

Anne Marie searched his eyes. He believed her, or at least wanted to.

"Why don't you start from the beginning."

"You mean everything?" Anne Marie asked, with a wave of her hand, implying since she'd moved here.

Danny nodded.

"Well." She gazed around the room and saw ghosts everywhere. "The cactus happened because Phil dropped it when he was helping me move."

"Phil? Is that the guy that was sitting out in the hall?"

"No, I think that was Jimmie."

Danny just looked at her.

"Phil is Judy's boyfriend. Anyway, there's nothing weird about the cactus, aside from the fact that it's turning yellow, but that just started, so...."

"Why do you haul it everywhere?"

"I told you. I took it to the nursery to get Milt's opinion about what to do for it."

"Milt?"

Anne Marie nodded. "I was bringing it back home when you saw me."

"And this thing with taking it up on the roof?"

"That's to give it sun."

"All right," Danny said. "So at least as far as the cactus goes, there's nothing out of the ordinary?"

"I don't think so, no. I've had it a long time though and it's obvious it's suffering. I'm worried about it. Milt says he thinks it's in shock."

"From being dropped?"

"Yes."

"And the pink dress?"

"That's a different story." She told him about buying it and why, thought again about the song lyrics, and wondered out loud. "Maybe I just thought I heard them on the phone. Maybe it was a wrong number and the person hung up and since I keep hearing that song anyway...."

"Why? Has something like that ever happened before?"

"No." Anne Marie shook her head. "But a lot of things have been happening that never happened before."

"Like what?"

"Like when I put the dress on and felt pregnant."

"What?"

Anne Marie nodded. "Miss Colorado said the girl before me was pregnant. The dress had been altered."

Danny shook his head and glanced at the door. "That's weird. How long have you known her?"

"Miss Colorado? Just since I moved here, why?"

"Just wondering."

"She's really nice," Anne Marie said somewhat defensively.

"I didn't say she wasn't."

Anne Marie looked at him.

"So what happens now when you put the dress on?"

"I don't know. I only wore it that one time. For a while I couldn't even be in the same room with it without getting sick, remember. Then all of a sudden, nothing. I got mad and said 'Talk to me, tell me what you want,' and nothing."

"Talk to me?" Danny raised an eyebrow.

"Come on, you know what I mean."

"No," Danny said, smiling. "I don't." He leaned close and kissed her. "But I do like it when you talk to me. Why don't you go put it on."

"What? The dress?"

"Yeah."

"Why?"

"To see what happens."

Anne Marie laughed. "Are you joking?"

"No."

He wasn't. He was serious.

"Just don't faint on me, okay?"

Anne Marie smiled and though generally shy, felt compelled to kiss him, and not once but twice. "I'll be right back."

"Wait." He held her hand to prevent her leaving. "How about if I order a pizza or something. I haven't eaten yet."

"All right." She shrugged.

"Sausage and pepperoni okay?"

Anne Marie nodded and went into the bedroom to change. "So far so good," she said a few minutes later when he asked how she was doing.

"Is it making you sick?"

"No." She walked out into the hall, paused, and decided to go back in and put on her heels. She brushed her hair then and put on some lipstick, a shade of pink almost the color of the dress, and dabbed perfume behind her ears and on her wrists. "There."

Danny was standing at the window overlooking the street as she entered the living room, turned at the sound of her rustling skirt, and paled.

"What?" Anne Marie said, from the look on his face. "What is it?"

"You, Anne Marie." He started toward her, but then stopped, and literally went weak in the knees. "I feel like I know you. I mean really know you, if you know what I mean."

"What? How can that be?"

"I don't know. But that baby you're carrying."

"Yes."

"I think I know who's responsible."

"You do? Who?"

"Me."

CHAPTER TWENTY-FIVE

"Who are you?"

Danny shook his head. He didn't know. All he knew at the moment was that she belonged to him, they belonged to one another, and that he wanted her.

"Hold me," Anne Marie whispered, responding.

Danny drew her into his arms and kissed her, their bodies becoming one in a familiar way, and there was a knock on the door.

They both stared. "It's probably the pizza," Danny said, suddenly feeling awkward and yawning as if awakening from a dream.

Anne Marie turned toward the kitchen. Plates, she'd have to get plates. And forks and napkins. She forced herself to think. What else? Drinks. They would need something to drink.

She heard the front door close, looked, and knew from the expression in Danny's eyes that whatever had come over him was gone and he was back to himself again. She smiled, but with some regret. That meant she was back as well, and they might never know.

"Do you have any children, Danny?" she asked.

He shook his head no.

Anne Marie stared inside the refrigerator. "Grape juice okay?"

"Fine."

"I think I'll go change first." She started past him.

"Don't," Danny said. "You look so nice."

"Yeah, well I feel stupid. Besides, it's gone anyway."

Danny put the pizza on the counter and reached for her. "Maybe it'll come back."

Anne Marie searched his eyes. One was bluer than the other, and sparkled more. Maybe, just maybe.... "Let's go up and eat on the roof."

"What?"

"The roof. The moon'll be out soon."

Danny smiled. "You're not going to bring the cactus, are you?"

"No." Anne Marie laughed and went for the blanket.

They brought plates and napkins along, two mugs and the bottle of grape juice, salt and pepper, and for dessert, raisins, because it was all the sweets she had. "I was going to make oatmeal bread," she told him in the elevator. "But I never got around to it."

"You dawdle," she could hear her mother say. "If you just managed your time a little better...."

Anne Marie shivered.

"Are you cold?" Danny asked.

"No." She was grateful when they were finally under the wide-open sky. Voices in her head had a way of getting lost in so much space. "Good, no one's here." She spread the blanket close to the wall, sat down cross-legged on the one side with her taffeta dress billowing around her like a ballerina's, and looked up at Danny. "Sit," she said, and he smiled.

The moon was but a crescent.

"Do you feel anything?" he asked.

Anne Marie shook her head. "Maybe if I wished upon a star."

Danny filled their cups and handed her one. "What would you wish for?"

"I don't know."

"All right," he said, making a toast. "To nothing."

Anne Marie echoed his sentiments. "To nothing."

They both helped themselves to pizza. Danny added lots of pepper to his, Anne Marie, salt, and the two of them settled into eating.

"This is good," Anne Marie said.

Danny nodded with a mouthful.

"Do you think they had pizza in the fifties?"

"I don't know. Why?"

Anne Marie shrugged. "Just wondering."

Danny smiled. She was always just wondering. "I think the thing would be to find out if they had pizza in New Orleans in the fifties."

"What?"

He laughed.

"Why?"

"Don't you remember when you asked me if I'd ever been to New Orleans? You said you were just wondering then too, just like now."

Anne Marie looked at him. "Do you think there's a connection?"

"No. I'm just wondering why you're always just wondering."

Anne Marie smiled, the lyrics of the song, "I wonder, wonder who...." playing through her mind. But then she came to the line, "Who wrote the book of love?" and her smile faded. "Ask me something else." she said.

"Why?" Danny put his pizza down. "Do you feel something?"

Anne Marie shook her head and laughed. "I don't think you should keep asking me that, okay?"

"Sorry," he said. "But this is all new to me."

"Me too." She touched the side of his face. "Me too. Why don't we just eat."

"Fine. Give me some raisins," he said, which had Anne Marie laughing again. "Hey, don't knock it till you try it," he told her, shaking some onto his pizza and taking a bite. "We might be on to something here."

"No thanks."

"You sure?"

"Positive." Anne Marie glanced around the roof in the twilight, the night warm and breezy, and was having such fun she started feeling guilty, what with everything going on in her life. On top of that, she glanced up at the moon just then and saw bats, at least a dozen of them swarming high above their heads, and cringed. "Oh God."

Danny followed her eyes and smiled. "They won't bother you."

"Oh sure." Anne Marie remembered a barn, a fleeting memory, with bats everywhere. The fluttering wings, the sound...and how frightened she was. But it wasn't her memory. She'd never been inside a barn in her life. It was the memory of someone else, there one moment and gone the next. She heard music then, knew the words to the song by heart, and turned to Danny. "Do you hear that?"

"The radio?" He nodded. "Yes."

"It's 'Tell Laura I Love Her.'"

"I know."

Anne Marie gazed into his eyes. "Would you dance with me, Danny?"

"Here?" he asked. "Now?"
"Yes," she said, and reached for his hand.

CHAPTER TWENTY-SIX

Anne Marie knocked on Miss Colorado's door, waited a moment, and knocked again. "Miss Colorado? Miss Colorado, are you home?" She wanted to tell her about last night, about how she and Danny danced on the roof under the stars and the moon, and about what he said. But if she were going to get to the hospital on time, walking, she'd have to leave now. She waited a few more minutes, then took the plate of warm oatmeal bread she'd baked early this morning back to her apartment, and left.

Her mother was sitting up in bed, makeup on, and hair sprayed stiff. "Well?"

Anne Marie sat down next to her. This was the plan, to sit by her side. "Do they do it here, or...?"

Her mother nodded.

Anne Marie glanced around the room. "Did the doctor explain exactly what they do? I mean...?" She envisioned a large machine, some sort of chemical immersion, where a body is radiated with poison, and....

"It's done intravenously," her mother said. "I'm told there's nothing to it."

Anne Marie stared. "How long does it take?"

"A few hours. Why? Do you have somewhere to go?"

Anne Marie hesitated. "No."

"Have you gotten another job?"

Anne Marie shook her head.

"Are you looking?"

Anne Marie paused, thought about lying just to make her happy, but it wasn't in her. "No, not really."

Her mother nodded, as if she'd figured as much, and made a hmph sound. "I plan on going out Monday," Anne Marie said, in an effort to end the subject.

Her mother nodded again. A technician entered the room then, along with two nurses and the hospital chaplain.

"Hello, Mrs. Light! How are you today?"

Anne Marie edged her chair back, their voices blending.

"Here's what we're going to do," one of them said.

"We're going to set up a shunt."

"We don't want to have to infiltrate you every time."

Anne Marie thought of a battle line. War.

"Your veins have a tendency to roll."

"Is this your daughter?"

Anne Marie raised her eyes.

"Yes."

"An only child?"

"Yes."

"How nice of you to be here for your mom."

Anne Marie didn't know what to say.

"I told her she didn't have to come." Her mother grimaced in pain as the technician's first effort to find a vein failed miserably. "She's not employed at the moment though, so...."

Both nurses turned their attention.

"I got fired," Anne Marie said, her response instinctual and reminiscent of other battles, many, many of them. "I have good timing."

"Anne Marie?" she heard a distant voice say. "Not now."

"I'm sorry, Grandmother. But Mom started it."

"Not today, hush. You hear me? Not today."

Anne Marie sighed. "I would be here no matter what."

The nurses smiled as her mother looked at her, feeling perhaps they were witnessing a sentimental moment. But right about then the technician jabbed another vein, and out came hostility. "I thought for once you were doing a good job."

The technician apologized.

"Not you," Anne Marie said, feeling sorry for the woman. "She meant me."

The chaplain stepped forward. "Shall we pray."

107

Oh Lord. Anne Marie bowed her head. Now I lay me down to sleep. This little light of mine, I'm going to let it shine. Zacchaeus, you come down, cause I'm going to your house today. Cause I'm going to your house today. Cause I'm going to your house today....

"Amen."

Anne Marie's memory reeled on and on. The Lord is my shepherd, I shall not want. Our Father who art in heaven. For God so loved the world.... "All set," she heard one of the nurses say. And when she raised her eyes, she and her mother were alone.

"What happened to your roommate?" Anne Marie asked, just then realizing the woman in the next bed was gone as well.

"She asked to be transferred yesterday," her mother said, staring at the needle in her arm. "My having cancer made her nervous."

"Why? It's not contagious. Did she tell you that?"

Her mother shook her head, still staring at the IV while keeping her arm as stiff as a board. "I overheard her telling her husband and he left right away, and...." Her mother drew a deep breath and leaned her head back. "You should have brought a camera."

"Why?"

"To take my picture. You could have titled it...."

Anne Marie smiled, remembering the summer she got her first very own 35mm, and how she took pictures of everything, even when she didn't have film, and titled each shot. And how mad her mother would get.

"Get that camera out of my face!"

"Say cheese."

"I mean it, young lady!"

Her mother laughed.

"What ever happened to that camera?"

"I buried it."

"What?"

Her mother nodded. "Out by the lilies. When I die, you can go dig it up."

Anne Marie smiled. "And the pictures?"

"Still in it."

The film would have depicted their last Christmas together, the day before Anne Marie moved out for good. She envisioned her mother burying it under the snow; the frozen ground no match for the power of her anger.

"Do you remember Missy?"

Anne Marie looked at her. Of course she remembered Missy. She loved that dog.

"There's pictures of her there too."

Anne Marie swallowed hard. "What do you mean?"

Her mother shrugged, as if reconsidering her decision to mention it, and seemed to find the answer in the slow drip of the IV. "It wasn't enough to say she was a cat, Anne Marie, I'm sorry. It just wasn't. But I want you to know I liked that dog too."

Sure, Anne Marie thought, that's why you took her to the pound after I spent days training her to use the litter box, and walking her at midnight so no one in the apartment would see her, and how I would talk to her and talk to her so she wouldn't bark, and bought her food with my own babysitting money and made sure to only buy cat food in case someone was watching, and how Missy seemed to like it, and....

"You scared me, Anne Marie. I thought you were losing your mind, and that maybe it was the allergy pills I took when I was pregnant with you."

Anne Marie smiled. "Mom, I knew she wasn't a cat."

Her mother looked at her, just looked at her for a moment, then shook her head. "Well, you could've fooled me, you and all your ridiculousness about dimensions and reality and perception and constantly going around saying here kitty, kitty and trying to teach the damned dog to meow. I thought...."

Anne Marie laughed. And for the second time today her mother even laughed. But then the IV machine started beeping and they grew quiet again, feeling responsible somehow, as the two of them waited solemnly for a nurse to come remedy the problem.

CHAPTER TWENTY-SEVEN

Anne Marie met Judy for lunch at the hot dog vendor's, and was so hungry, she ordered two super-deluxes. Judy was amazed. Her best friend as a rule was not a big eater. "What's with you?"

"I don't know." Anne Marie smiled. "It's probably all the walking." The two of them headed for the curb in front of the newsstand, sat down, and stretched their legs out.

"How's your mom?"

"Okay." Anne Marie paused. "They said it usually takes a couple of days to start having side effects."

Judy nodded, saying how Greta Lupinski, her favorite soap opera actress, underwent chemotherapy on the show. "Is she going to lose her hair?" Greta Lupinski did.

"The doctor says he doesn't know, because not everyone on the dose she's getting does."

"It grows back, even so."

"I know." Anne Marie tossed the last bite of her first hot dog to a very patient pigeon, shooed the others when they came rushing, and started on her next. "I made the oatmeal bread, you'll have to come get yours."

"What about tonight?" Judy said. "What time did you say your telephone man was picking you up?"

Anne Marie laughed. "Oh no, he's just now getting used to me. Why don't you come this afternoon."

"What, walking? No thanks. I'll have Phil drive me over before he goes to work. When will you be there?"

Anne Marie glanced at the sun; it was almost directly overhead. Noon. She smiled to herself, wondering when it was she started telling time by the sky. Since the day she walked to her mother's, she decided, and gauged the time needed to get home if she took the long way.

"Well?"

"I don't know. Around four." They made plans to see each other then, and Anne Marie set out in that general direction. She first passed the tract of stores burned in the fire, nothing had been done with them as of yet; they were still boarded up. Then she walked to where her old apartment building used to be, stopped long enough to notice a tiny tomato sprout growing smack dab in the center of the desolate lot, and picked up her pace. Two little girls were playing hopscotch in the middle of the sidewalk when she finally made the turn onto her street, and looked so much like her and Judy at their age, she tiptoed around them for fear they'd vanish before her eyes.

"Hey, how's it going?" her veteran neighbor asked from the stoop, where he sat drinking a beer.

"Okay," Anne Marie said, catching her breath and mopping her brow.

"You training for a marathon or something?"

"No." Anne Marie smiled, gripping his shoulder for support as she started up the steps past him. "I'm just saving money."

"Tough racket," he said, nodding, and turned to look at her. "Do you cut hair?"

"What?"

"Do you cut hair? I need a hair cut."

Anne Marie laughed. The man had hair down to his shoulders, thick and wavy and with a healthy shine. "Your hair looks good. Leave it alone."

"Thanks," he said.

Anne Marie smiled, pushed the door open to the hall, and froze. A man was sitting on the floor outside her apartment. And it wasn't Jimmie.

She backed up, let the door ease shut, and looked at the veteran.

"He's been there for hours," her neighbor said, as if reading her mind. "Who is it anyway?"

"I don't know." Anne Marie shook her head. The man was big and bulky, and red. Blood red.

"I take it you don't want to talk to him."

"I...." Anne Marie stammered. "I don't like the looks of him."

The veteran gazed at her and chuckled. "Then you better hurry and hide, cause I hear him coming."

Anne Marie hesitated for a split second, then ran down the stairs and around to the alley on the side.

"Hey, how's it going?" she heard her veteran neighbor say.

And a reply. "Go to hell."

She peeked around the corner, recognizing the voice, and gasped. It was her father. "Dad?"

The man walked away, his back to her.

"Dad?"

He kept walking.

"Did you say that was your dad?" The veteran cocked an eyebrow. "Nice guy."

Anne Marie swallowed hard as she stared down the empty street, no little girls playing hopscotch. "He's dead."

The veteran turned and stared in the same direction a moment. "Far out."

Anne Marie looked at him, long and hard, and shook her head. He saw ghosts all the time, why should it bother him to see one of hers. She started back up the steps, glanced once more down the street, and went inside and knocked on Miss Colorado's door.

There was no answer.

"Miss Colorado? Miss Colorado, are you home?"

Silence.

Anne Marie drew a deep breath and raked her fingers through her damp hair. It wasn't the end of the world, her seeing her dead father. She used to see him all the time, though never like this. What concerned her more at this point was Miss Colorado. Where would the woman go, all day yet? And if she was home, why wasn't she answering her door?

CHAPTER TWENTY-EIGHT

Judy didn't understand Anne Marie's anxiety over this Miss Colorado's absence, but didn't have time for an explanation. Phil was honking his horn. "I'm sorry. I gotta go."

Anne Marie nodded, watched the door open and close, and commenced pacing. How long had she known the little woman? Certainly not long enough to care this much, she tried telling herself. And certainly not enough to know for sure that it would be odd she not be home for a day.

No. She recalled what Miss Colorado said about not going shopping, how she didn't like people staring at her, making fun and laughing. And the woman couldn't really see to begin with, someone would have had to guide her, take her with them, maybe against her will, and....

Anne Marie glanced at the clock on the kitchen stove, decided she needed to stretch out under the sun, even if only for a little while, and took the cactus with her. Calm down, she kept telling herself, you need to calm down. What a relief finally to be alone, just her and the sun and the cactus, the world as distant as the muffled sounds of traffic below.

Relax.... Relax....

Eyes closed, she opened her palms to the warmth of the descending rays, drew a deep breath, and held it. Don't count, she could hear her grandmother say, your body will tell you when. No rules, no numbers. Let it out. Now breathe again, breathe deep, hold it...and exhale. Again....

"Grandmother. Grandmother, I saw him again."

"Breathe...."

"I don't remember him like that."

"Breathe...."

Anne Marie listened to the sound of her grandmother's voice, farther and farther away, softer and softer, and drifted with her hand resting on the base of the cactus.

"Here she is! I found her!"

Anne Marie rolled sleepily onto her side.

"She's right here!"

"What?" Anne Marie looked up and found herself staring into Miss Congeniality's anxious face. "Who?"

The young woman reached across her and picked up a shimmering black cat, cuddled it to her breast, and turned with tears of relief as her companion came rushing to them.

"Is she all right? Is she all right?"

Anne Marie sat up dazed as she glanced from one to the other, and wondered how the cat got there, what path it took.

"Look at her. She's not even scared."

The cat purred up a storm.

"She was all curled up, sleeping."

Anne Marie smiled and looked in the direction of the setting sun, all but gone now. Seven, seven-fifteen, she thought, and checked the wrist of first the one woman, then the other. "What time is it, please?"

"Ten after seven," the normally not-so-friendly one said, sniffling and then blushing as she wiped at her eyes. "Thank you."

Anne Marie nodded, thanking her as well, and the two women walked away fussing and cooing to the cat, saying how worried they were and about to have heart attacks, you have to stop doing this.

"How long has she been gone?" Anne Marie asked.

"All day," the one said.

"We thought we'd never see her again."

"We don't know how she gets out."

The elevator door closed with its customary creak and bang, but not before both women waved and thanked her again, and Anne Marie turned to the cactus.

"We have to hurry, or I'm going to be late," she said, and took the stairs to save time. Danny was due in less than an hour and she didn't even know what she was going to wear.

Jeans?

No, he said they were going someplace nice.

So? What's wrong with jeans?

She laughed. That was *her* saying that. And jeans it was. She laid everything out on the bed, jeans, socks, underwear and bra, sweater and blazer, and rummaged through the bottom of her closet for just the right shoes. "There." She decided on a pair of brown oxfords, worn, but still in decent shape, and went in to take a bath.

The hot water felt good on her tired legs, weary from all the miles, and tingly on her breasts. She wished she had hours, days, to just lie there, the water cresting her chin, and slid under completely to consume it all in just seconds, the water ebbing still against her skin as she listened to the silence.

Thoughts of Jimmie entered her mind then and traveled down through her body, no matter how hard she tried to force them away, thoughts of the beginning, his arms around her, his mouth on hers, and she surfaced, aching inside.

She thought about the time they painted each other's faces with watercolors, and how she insisted they paint by candlelight, so she wouldn't see his colors change on their own. She thought about the night they moved in together, how he carried her across the threshold, and the way he looked in the morning, his hair all mussed and his eyes sultry.

She drew a breath and sighed. "You're dawdling," she could hear her mother say. And for once, she agreed. She hurried and bathed, washed her hair, rinsed it until it squeaked, and got out and dried. Danny was going to be here any minute now, and no matter what, she was going to be ready.

CHAPTER TWENTY-NINE

Danny smiled all over. "You look so pretty," he said to Anne Marie, and kissed her.

"Thank you. You look pretty nice yourself." He had on dress slacks, a dress shirt and tie, and a brown leather bomber jacket, which used to be his brother's, he said, and the only thing left of him.

"How old was he?"

"Twenty-two."

Anne Marie watched the sadness come and go behind his eyes.

"Do you like Japanese food?"

"I don't know. I guess so." She couldn't remember ever having had any. Chinese food maybe, but not Japanese.

"Good, I made reservations at the Samurai."

Anne Marie pictured two sumo wrestlers in a kitchen, head-locking one another, pushing and shoving, then wielding swords. "Have you eaten there before?" she asked.

"Yeah, it's great. You'll love it."

Anne Marie smiled hopefully, glanced at the cactus before leaving and hesitated in the hall, wondering if she dare try Miss Colorado one more time. She weighed the possibilities. If there was no answer as before, she'd think about it all night and start worrying all over again. But maybe if she just turned and walked away, she'd be able to convince herself that if she had checked, Miss Colorado would have finally been home, safe and sound, and let it rest. And perhaps....

Danny looked at her. "What's the matter?"

"Miss Colorado. She hasn't been home all day."

"So?"

"So...." Anne Marie frowned. "I think it's odd. I'm worried about her."

Danny smiled. "Maybe she's visiting her family."

Anne Marie shook her head. "I don't think she has any."

"Okay, friends then."

Anne Marie shrugged. She didn't know if she had any of them either. Wouldn't a friend do her shopping for her? Why would she have to pay someone? "I'm sorry." She apologized to Danny for the delay, and went and knocked on the door.

"Miss Colorado? Miss Colorado, are you home?"

She heard rustling from inside, waited, and knocked again.

Danny walked up next to her. "Maybe she's sleeping."

Anne Marie glanced at him, shook her head, and pressed her ear against the door. "Miss Colorado?" She thought she heard some rustling again, but then nothing.

"Come on," Danny said, convincing her, and the two left. There was a threat of rain, so they rode across town with the T-tops in, and didn't have much to say. When the news came on the radio, Anne Marie immediately turned it off.

Danny looked at her. "We don't have to go, Anne Marie. I mean if you're that worried."

"No, it's okay." She stared out the window. "You're right. I don't really know if she has family. Maybe she does. Or maybe she did just go out for the day."

"We'll check again when we get back. We don't have to stay late."

Anne Marie nodded. He was so nice, so understanding, he was almost too good to be true. Jimmie would be having a fit, raising hell and calling her paranoid as usual, and....

Danny pulled into the restaurant and parked, didn't turn off the car right away, and sat revving the engine slightly.

"What's the matter?" Anne Marie asked.

He turned the lights off and then turned them back on again. "Nothing," he said, smiling, but revved the engine again anyway for some reason.

It sounded fine to Anne Marie, and apparently Danny was satisfied as well then, because he turned it off, and got out and came around and opened her door. "I hope you're hungry," he said, reaching for her hand. "They feed you to death here."

The restaurant was dark and mysterious, with brightly colored dragons everywhere. "Right this way."

Anne Marie followed a "geisha girl" through a maze, still holding onto Danny's hand, and was asked to remove her shoes outside a small room. "Wow..." she said, and Danny laughed. He removed his shoes as well, and they were ushered into their own private dining room, a sunken table in the center, with cushions all around, and sat down across from one another in the candlelight.

"This place is amazing," Anne Marie whispered.

"I know." Danny smiled. "Wait till you taste the food."

Anne Marie leaned back as the geisha girl placed a tiny cup of warm wine in front of her. "Saki," she said, waiting for Anne Marie's approval. "You taste."

"Thank you." Anne Marie took a sip. "It's very good."

The geisha girl smiled a porcelain smile, placed a cup in front of Danny, and bowed as she backed out of the room.

"Wow!" Anne Marie said again. "I feel like I'm in another world."

Danny smiled. "I always feel that way around you," he said, and laughed when Anne Marie shook her head. "I mean it," he added, growing serious.

She turned away.

"Anne Marie...." He waited for her to look at him.

"Yes."

"Can it just be you and me tonight? Can we do that?"

Anne Marie smiled a tentative smile. "If everyone else is in agreement."

Danny laughed.

"Cheers."

CHAPTER THIRTY

At eleven that night, Miss Colorado finally answered her door. "I'm sorry if I woke you," Anne Marie said.

"No, that's okay, dear. I was awake. Who's that?" She peered without her glasses at the shadow to Anne Marie's left.

"It's Danny," Anne Marie said. "The telephone man."

Danny rolled his eyes.

"We were out for dinner. Are you all right?"

"Yes, dear, fine. Why?"

"I was worried. I was by several times, and when you didn't answer...."

"Today?"

Anne Marie nodded, then remembered she couldn't really see her. "Yes, three times."

"Oh my," Miss Colorado said. "That's strange, I've been home all day."

Anne Marie glanced at Danny, standing patiently at her side. "I knocked, didn't I?"

His expression changed from lighthearted tolerance to one of concern. "Of course you did."

Anne Marie sighed a sigh of relief. "Well, I'm sorry to bother you," she told Miss Colorado. "But wait, one minute and I'll be right back. I made oatmeal bread and I want you to have some for breakfast."

"How lovely. Thank you."

Danny trailed after Anne Marie into her apartment, smiled when she said she'd only be a second, and walked over to the CD player. "Where are the CDs?" he asked, as she headed out.

"Nowhere. I don't have any."

Danny nodded, looked around, and went over and sat down on the couch to wait. He stood when Anne Marie returned, and followed her with his eyes as she walked right past him and into the bathroom.

"What's the matter? Are you okay?"

"Fine," she said, sounding as if she were underwater.

"Anne Marie?" She'd left the door open in her haste, and was obviously at the sink, so he went to see for himself. "What's wrong?"

She raised her head and looked at him in the mirror, her face dripping wet from splashing cold water on it. "I didn't have one visitor today, apparently I had two."

"What?"

"Two." She splashed more water on her face, cupped her hands over her nose and mouth to try and calm herself, and reached for the towel.

Danny handed it to her. "What do you mean, visitors?"

Anne Marie hesitated. "Well for one, Jimmie."

"The guy the other day?"

Anne Marie nodded.

"Who else?"

Anne Marie heard the voices in her head. "Don't tell him. Keep it to yourself. Don't do it. Do you hear me? Don't tell him."

"Anne Marie?"

She looked at him. How could she explain? It was one thing for her to see her dead father, and even the veteran for that matter, after all he'd been through. But Miss Colorado? How could she possibly see him too? The man was dead. Dead.

"Deader than a doornail," she remembered overhearing her mother say. "The no-good son of a bitch."

"Anne Marie? Who?"

"My father," she said, omitting the fact that he was long gone. "Let's just forget it, okay?" She felt awkward being in the bathroom with him, even though he was only standing in the doorway, and started out past him. "I don't want to talk about it."

"Fine."

The next thing she knew, she was in his arms, crying, and all because he'd stepped out of her way but had also kindly reached for her hand.

"It's all right," he said. "It's all right."

120

"No it's not. You don't understand."

"Understand what?"

"I can't tell you."

"Then you're right," Danny said, turning her face so she would look at him. "I don't understand."

Anne Marie wiped her eyes and smiled. "I'm sorry."

"Me too. Now what's the problem?"

"I don't know." Anne Marie softened in his embrace, color flushing her cheeks. "I lost my job, for one."

Danny kissed her.

"My mom is sick."

Danny kissed her again.

"My dad is dead."

Danny nuzzled her neck. "I thought you said you saw him today."

"I did. Sorta."

Danny lifted his head and gazed at her. "What do you mean?"

Anne Marie hesitated, not wanting to lie. "I don't know. Maybe it wasn't him. Maybe it was someone that just looked like him."

"At your door?" Danny said.

Fresh tears flooded Anne Marie's eyes. It was no use. "I used to see him all the time, though never like this."

"In your mind, you mean?"

Anne Marie shrugged. "But how could Miss Colorado see him?"

"I don't know. Are you sure he's dead?"

"No." Anne Marie tried to remember the day. She was twelve and it was summer. "I wasn't there. My mother wouldn't let me."

"And you say she's sick?"

Anne Marie nodded, comforted that he'd listened, that he didn't turn and run or tell her she was crazy. His eyes were kinder and bluer than ever. "Do you ever get scared, Danny?"

"About what?" he asked, holding her closer.

"I don't know. Anything."

"Sure." When she looked up at him expectantly, he added, "I was afraid earlier the car wouldn't start."

"What?" Anne Marie laughed and wiped her eyes.

"I'm serious," he said, with that grin of his. "I don't know what the hell's wrong with it. I replaced the alternator, it's got a new battery, I checked all the wires, I went over everything, and it's still not charging right."

Anne Marie shook her head. She wasn't sure if he was making this up or just telling her this to make her feel better, but either way it worked. "I had such a nice time tonight. Thank you."

"You're welcome," he said, and motioned to the door as a way of asking if he should go.

"No...."

"Then wait," Danny said, pulling away reluctantly. "I don't want there to be any misunderstanding." He went to her closet, found the prom dress and took it out into the living room, then reached for her hand. And Anne Marie smiled.

CHAPTER THIRTY-ONE

Anne Marie walked to the hospital to sit with her mom, day two, and met her new roommate, a woman who liked to talk and who had fiery red hair and no eyebrows.

"No toenails either," her mother whispered.

"What?"

"No toenails," she mouthed, leaning back behind the curtain so the woman couldn't see her pointing. "Look."

Anne Marie didn't want to gawk but felt compelled, her mother was so insistent, and sure enough, she was right. No toenails. Just toes.

"I was telling your mom earlier about my operation." The woman's gallbladder had been removed. "What a doctor. If it weren't for him, I would be dead. See, I'm already eating soft foods. What a practitioner. And HMO covered everything. What kind of insurance do you have, Rebecca?"

Anne Marie's mind wandered, if she could only remember the details of that day. If only someone would tell her.

"Mom?"

Rebecca Light looked at her, scolding her with her eyes for interrupting. "What?"

This better be good, young lady, she used to say.

"Well?"

"How did Dad die?"

Her mother sighed. "Oh, Anne Marie, really," she said, her expression loud and clear.

"I was just wondering."

"Why? Because *I'm* dying?"

Her neighbor gasped. "Oh, Rebecca, are you? I'm sorry. Who's your doctor? Maybe...."

Anne Marie retreated deep inside herself, their voices echoing from far, far away. "You're not dying, Mom."

"What? Don't you dare start that."

"I'm sorry, but you're not."

Her mother looked at her. "You're sorry? What do you mean you're sorry? What's that supposed to mean?"

Anne Marie heard her grandmother laugh. "Oh you two," she said, and it was because her grandmother's laugh was so infectious, that Anne Marie laughed.

"It's just a feeling, Mom. I have a feeling you're not going to die. Not now I mean."

Her mother shook her head and glanced at her roommate. "She has a feeling."

The woman smiled. She too had a feeling, she said, a good one. Rebecca was going to be just fine, praise be to God, that it probably just wasn't her time, she still had something left to do. "And like I was just this morning telling my doctor...."

Anne Marie stared out the window and remembered the phone ringing, but that was all. She left for school and wasn't told until that afternoon when she returned home. She recalled thinking it odd her mother hadn't gone to work, she never missed work. And she wasn't sick, so....

"Your father's dead."

"How, Mom?"

Her mother looked at her. "Why bring this up now?"

Anne Marie shook her head. She could only imagine the fit her mother would throw if she said she saw him sitting outside her door.

"What's the point?"

Anne Marie shrugged. "There is no point. Forget it." She glanced out the window and noticed a funeral procession. Don't count the cars, she told herself, and crammed a bunch of out of sequence numbers in her head to ward off the temptation. "Can I get you anything?"

Her mother said no and moaned deep down.

"Are you in pain?"

"A little," Rebecca admitted begrudgingly, gripping her side. "It's the stitches, I guess."

Her neighbor sympathized. "When I had my hysterectomy, the pain was terrible. Of course I had a different doctor then, who I don't mind saying didn't care a whole lot for his patients. I only saw him once after the surgery, but got a bill that said he was in to see me three times. Well, needless to say I called the office right that very minute, and...."

Anne Marie lowered her eyes to the floor and stared, the room falling deathly silent around her but for the steady drip of the IV. And it wasn't until she heard her mother stir, that she looked up to see her smiling at something her roommate had said.

Now. Now was the time to ask, while she was in a good mood. Ask, she told herself. Ask. But she couldn't. She swallowed hard and instead, just listened as the two women talked, their exchange soft and friendly as she stared out the window.

"Anne Marie?"

She turned and saw her grandmother standing at the head of the bed. "Ask her. Ask her what you need to know."

"I can't," Anne Marie said in her mind. "She'll get mad."

"No, she won't. Not anymore."

Anne Marie drew a deep breath, and wasn't so sure. "The last time I asked, I got slapped across the face. Remember, you were there."

"Yes, and what did you learn from that?"

"I don't know. That I should've ducked?"

Her grandmother's laughter again filled the room. "Ask her. But ask her right this time."

Anne Marie decided to give it a try, but waited until the treatment was over and just before she was ready to leave. "Mom?" she said, lowering her voice so as not to be overheard.

"Yes." Her mother looked at her.

"Why did you change our names?"

"Why?"

Her grandmother was right. She didn't get mad this time. She didn't even flinch. And maybe she would have explained back then, had Anne Marie not gone down to the courthouse and asked questions there first.

"I wanted you to know we didn't need him, that we could stand on our own."

"Was Dad aware?"

125

Her mother shook her head. "He would have had to call or something to find out."

"And he never did?"

"No."

Anne Marie hesitated as a nurse entered the room to remove the IV. "What about the Christmas gifts? The birthday cards?"

Her mother shrugged.

They'd come from all over the country, and were always something Anne Marie really, really wanted. The semi-precision roller skates, just the right size. The mohair sweater. The AM/FM transistor radio. "How did he know?"

"He didn't." Her mother winced when the nurse accidentally bumped the shunt in her arm, and soured. "Don't you have more important things to think about? Did you find a job?"

"No."

"Then go. Maybe you can find one this afternoon."

Anne Marie nodded, dismissed as usual, and walked toward the door to leave but stopped and looked back. "He is dead, isn't he?"

Her mother glared at her in what appeared to be anger or perhaps disgust before turning away, and it was then Anne Marie noticed she was close to tears. "I'm sorry," Anne Marie said, though she had no idea why she was apologizing. "I didn't mean to...."

"Just go, Anne Marie. All right? Just go," Rebecca said, and Anne Marie would have, had her grandmother not still been standing there.

"Say something. Say something. Don't go like this."

"Uh...I forgot to tell you," Anne Marie said.

Her mother looked at her.

"I went out with Danny again last night?"

Her mother brightened instantly. "The telephone man?"

"Yes. We went to dinner."

Her mother reached for a tissue. "Where?"

"The Samurai."

"Oh, that's a nice place," her roommate said. "And expensive."

"We're going out again tonight. I'll tell you all about it tomorrow." If the doctors were right, tomorrow her mother was going to start feeling the effects of the chemo and would need a diversion. "We're going bowling with some friends of his."

Rebecca smiled. "Wear some makeup."

"What?"

"Some makeup."

Anne Marie shook her head and took leave while her mother was still happy. She'd promised Judy she'd stop by on the way home, and walked along thinking about last night, start to finish and ending in Danny's arms, warm and weak and gloriously wet.

Judy was waiting for her on the steps.

"What?" Anne Marie said, from her expression.

"Phil's sleeping."

"So." Sitting outside was fine with Anne Marie; there wasn't a cloud in the sky. "Let him sleep."

Judy nodded, glancing anxiously at her best friend, and hesitated before fishing into her pocket for something. "Jimmie was here," she said, handing her a note. "He said to give this to you."

Anne Marie leveled her eyes on the sealed envelope, took it when she noticed Judy's hand trembling, and stared at the name Anne in Jimmie's familiar handwriting.

"He says he needs an answer."

Anne Marie looked at her.

"By tonight."

CHAPTER THIRTY-TWO

Miss Colorado seemed rather disoriented. "Oh my," she kept saying, in response to no matter what. "I do remember something about that."

Anne Marie sipped her tea, a different potion this time, and asked about the blend.

"Oh my, let me think. I do remember...."

Anne Marie wondered about her age, which was difficult to tell, her being so tiny and child-like, and worried she might possibly have had a stroke or something. They'd talked about her mother, and even a little about her date with Danny, but for the most part, Miss Colorado was out of it. Nothing was registering. Upon leaving, Anne Marie decided to check on her later and this time, greatly relieved, found her to be herself again.

"Where are you off to, dear?" she asked.

"To fill out an application. There was an ad in the paper and...." If she'd calculated correctly, she'd have just enough time to get there and back before Danny arrived.

"What type of job is it?"

Anne Marie stole a quick glance at Miss Colorado's wristwatch. Five-ten. She'd have to hurry. "A kind of secretarial position, with some bookkeeping. I don't like accounting, but at this point I can't be choosy. I'll tell you all about it when...."

"Speaking of jobs, did I ever tell you about the time I was hired as a porn queen?"

"What?" Anne Marie's mouth dropped.

"A porn queen," Miss Colorado said matter-of-factly. "It was the year I turned eighteen."

Anne Marie found herself sitting back down.

"It was a very difficult time for me," Miss Colorado said, pausing. "More tea, dear?"

Anne Marie held out her cup. "Yes, please."

"The man said I had star quality. He said he could see it in my eyes, and asked if I'd ever dreamed of being a dancer?"

Anne Marie shook her head. She couldn't imagine any of this.

"Of course then when they finally got around to showing me a script, I didn't know what to do. I'd already packed and snuck away, so...."

"What *did* you do?"

"Well, for a while I just sat there, then I excused myself to go to the ladies room, and heard them talking. My being picked had nothing to do with my eyes. With pigtails, they said, I'd look just like a little girl."

Anne Marie felt sick to her stomach, which is how Miss Colorado said she felt at the time. There was no window to sneak out of though, and where would she go if she did? She was in a strange town, didn't know anybody.

"So I lied. I came out and told them I'd gotten my monthly, a really bad one, and even cut myself down there in case they didn't believe me, and swore I'd be back in five days."

Anne Marie smiled. "And by then you were...?"

"Back with the circus and long gone."

Anne Marie drank the rest of her tea and swirled the leaves in the bottom of her cup. There wasn't enough to form a distinct pattern, but with a stretch of the imagination her grandmother always said was necessary anyway, she saw a tree, one side with leaves and one without.

"Look," she said to Miss Colorado, who donned her glasses and smiled when she immediately saw it too.

"You'd better hurry, dear, if you're going to go apply for that job."

Anne Marie yawned. "I think I'll wait until tomorrow and go take a nap. The tea's making me sleepy."

The prom dress was on the chair in the living room where Danny had left it; he'd obviously taken care so it wouldn't wrinkle. And it was the last thing Anne Marie saw as she laid down on the couch and closed her eyes.

A knock on the door woke her.

"Anne?"

She froze.

"Anne, come on. I know you're in there."

How, she wondered? How do you know?

"Come on, I need to talk to you? Didn't you get my note?"

It was still in her jacket.

She heard another voice then, one she didn't recognize, then the sound of diminishing footsteps, and ultimate silence. The next time she woke, was to a woman's voice.

"Tell Laura I love her."

She opened her eyes.

"Tell her...."

The dress was gone.

She looked everywhere. The kitchen, the bedroom, the bathroom. The store where she bought it.

It was nowhere to be found. As she lay back down, exhausted from her search, she heard a distant bell ringing. "I'm going to be late for class," she told herself, which was nothing new, and dreamt she fell asleep again.

When Danny arrived, she was hardly rested, but did hear him knock, and was relieved to see the dress back. She must have imagined its disappearance, she decided, but stopped cold at the door with a sudden realization. The store she'd searched hadn't been the same, regardless of the fire and destruction. It was entirely different.

"Do you know the area code for New Orleans?" she asked Danny.

"No, why?" he said, wrapping her in his arms and kissing her.

"Can you get it?"

He nodded, again asking why. "What do you need it for?"

Anne Marie questioned her mind, trying to sort out what was real and what wasn't, but distinctly remembered the name over the door, and couldn't.... "I need to know if there's a store called Angela's Fashions. If I'm right, it's going to be on Magazine Street. 555 Magazine Street."

"Now?"

"Yes. Please."

Danny went into the bathroom to phone information, returned a few minutes later, and found Anne Marie sitting next to the cactus in the window, staring out into the night.

"Anne Marie?"

She turned and looked at him.

"There is one, but they're closed," he said. "The recording says they'll be open again Tuesday at nine."

Anne Marie nodded, thanking him. It was time to leave. "Do you want your jacket?" Danny asked, when she glanced back and hesitated.

"No." If she had it with her, she might be tempted to read Jimmie's note. "Not tonight," she said, and locked the door behind them.

CHAPTER THIRTY-THREE

Anne Marie was not a bowler, but had fun anyway. Danny's friends Joe and Rose, laughed and joked a lot, made her feel comfortable, and she even got two strikes in the third game. Danny on the other hand was very good, and she liked watching him. He was so precise, approaching the alley the same way each time, holding the ball a certain way. And the beer was ice cold. With a promise to get together again real soon, the two couples were rather mellow as they called it a night and walked to their cars.

"Ah shit," Danny said, after he turned the key and got a growl and a moan instead of ignition. He tried it again and when the same thing happened, got out and raised the hood.

"Go ahead," he told Anne Marie, motioning for her to turn the key.

Nothing.

"Wait, wait...hold on a minute," he said, and jiggled and moved something else. "All right, try it now."

The engine cranked, roared to a start, and it wasn't long before they were back at Anne Marie's. "Here, I bought you something," Danny said, having almost forgotten. It was two CDs, a Kenny G and Classic Oldies.

Anne Marie decided to play the Kenny G one first, which had no sooner started when she heard a door slam out in the hall, and frantic and familiar shouting.

"Medic! Medic!"

Oh no, she thought, not now, and felt embarrassed for the veteran.

"What the hell?" Danny looked at her.

"He was in Vietnam," she said. "He doesn't know he does this, I don't think."

The veteran started banging on doors.

"Don't!" Anne Marie said, when Danny headed across the room to answer hers. "He'll stop."

"When?" he asked, as if he couldn't stand a second more.

"I don't know. A couple of hours, sometimes longer."

Danny's eyes widened. Not tonight. He opened the door, looked both ways, and held his ground when the veteran came charging. "Incoming! Incoming!" the man shouted. And Danny cold-cocked him.

"Oh my God!" Anne Marie screamed.

"Oh my God!" Miss Colorado echoed, having appeared in the hall from behind her door at practically the same time. "What's going on? What's going on?"

"Danny punched the veteran."

"What!? Why?"

"To give him a break," Danny said, motioning for Anne Marie to show him which apartment was his. He picked him up by his arms then and dragged him inside, with Miss Colorado right behind them, clinging to Anne Marie and asking again and again why?

"He never hurt anyone. Why?"

"He'll be fine," Danny said, each and every time. "He'll be fine." He hoisted the veteran onto his couch and stuffed a pillow under his head. "He won't know what hit him."

Anne Marie led Miss Colorado back to her apartment and stayed with her a moment to make sure she was calmed down and breathing normally again and Danny went back to Anne Marie's. He was at the kitchen sink getting a drink of water when she returned, and couldn't understand what all the fuss was about.

"Would you rather he run around for two hours freaking out?"

"No, but...."

"But what?"

Anne Marie hesitated. "Miss Colorado says I'll probably get evicted."

"Why?"

"His dad owns the building."

"You're kidding?" Danny started to laugh.

"No, and I don't think it's funny. Finding this apartment wasn't exactly easy. I can see it all now. And where do you work? Uh...nowhere."

Danny laughed again and reached for her. "Come on. You can come live with me."

"No thank you," Anne Marie said, attempting to pull away and shaking her head. "I can't believe you did that."

"Yeah? Well I can't believe people let it happen," he said, and meant it.

Anne Marie searched the depths of his eyes, which bared his soul, and found herself warming in his arms. He honestly felt he'd done the right thing. "Do you really think he'll be all right?"

Danny nodded.

"I'm still going to check on him in the morning."

"You do that," he said, and kissed her.

"Early."

Danny smiled. "Don't wake me."

"I won't."

CHAPTER THIRTY-FOUR

Danny was right. Perched on his windowsill at six the following morning, drinking his freshly-ground coffee and dangling his bare feet, the veteran seemed fine. There wasn't even any swelling where Danny had punched him, that Anne Marie could see, without staring to be sure, and she got a cup of delicious coffee to boot.

When she returned to her apartment and crawled back into bed with Danny, he snuggled her close. The sun was just now peeking through the window, a sliver of a ray, but enough to illuminate the tattoo on his arm and she studied it up close. The red eyes, the black wings, the gray talons.

"Were you angry when you had this done?"

"At the world," he said, half asleep.

Anne Marie closed her eyes, lulled by the rhythm of his breathing, and could easily have fallen back to sleep herself, but had to leave for the hospital soon. When Danny woke she was taking a quick bath, and smiled at him when he appeared in the doorway in his jockey shorts. "The phone's over there, sir," she said, and he laughed.

"No thanks, lady. I've been here before."

Anne Marie threw water at him. "There's coffee made, I'll be out in a minute. And by the way," she called after him when he turned like a zombie and headed in that direction. "The veteran's fine."

Danny mumbled something she couldn't quite make out, and was dressed himself when she emerged ready to go. "Are you sure you don't want me to drive you?"

She nodded and moved the cactus to the far corner of the window so it would get the most morning sun, and reached for her jacket. "Yes, I need the exercise," she said, and also the miles and miles of time it would take to get there. She was dreading today, for her mother's sake, and for her own.

Her anxiety proved unwarranted, at first. Her mother was sitting up in bed, makeup on and hair combed to perfection as usual, and chatting with a new roommate.

"What happened to the woman yesterday?" Anne Marie asked.

"She was discharged."

"What a doctor," Anne Marie said.

Her mother chuckled. "She's going to come visit me tomorrow."

Anne Marie nodded. That didn't surprise her. Her mom made instant and very loyal friends. They flocked around her. The only people she usually alienated was family.

"Did you find a job?"

Anne Marie stared. "No."

"Did you look in the paper?"

"Yes."

"Today's?"

"No, not yet." Anne Marie hated her mom when she was like this, hated her....

"Well, how was your date?"

"Fine," Anne Marie said, erecting a great big wall between them.

"Aren't you going to tell me about it?"

"There's nothing to tell. We went bowling, his car wouldn't start and then it did, and we came home."

"What do you mean, his car wouldn't start?"

Anne Marie hesitated; her mother had a way of making everything sound so suspect. "There's something wrong with it and he can't figure it out. He rebuilt it himself."

Her mother scowled. "And apparently not very well."

"It runs beautifully," Anne Marie said, in a defensive tone.

"Right, it just doesn't start."

Anne Marie looked out the window. "It started."

The chaplain entered the room then in what appeared to be a huge rush to say hello and bless the patients. Divine intervention, Anne Marie mused, and looked around for her grandmother. She could picture her nudging the man down the hall, saying hurry, hurry, and practically shoving him through the door. When the thought of that made her laugh, everyone turned to see what was so funny.

136

"Nothing," Anne Marie said, and her mother sighed.

A collective moment of silence followed, one Anne Marie would recall again and again as she walked home. It wasn't like her to dwell on other people's reactions. Even as a child she was able to shrug them off. But not today for some reason.

She watched her feet hit the ground.

"Anne?"

She turned, startled, saw Jimmie, and started running. He was following her. Why was he following her? And with not one woman trailing behind him, but three.

"Wait! Wait!"

Anne Marie ducked into an alley, watched all four go whizzing by, and held her breath. Her father passed then, huffing and puffing. A dog running after him. And a whole bunch of strangers.

"No," she cried deep inside. "No." But they just kept coming. One after another. Again and again and again. Even when she closed her eyes and couldn't cry anymore. They just kept coming.

CHAPTER THIRTY-FIVE

Miss Colorado listened without a word. She didn't offer advice, interrupt or condemn, she just listened, and as usual, a special brew was conjured up to soothe Anne Marie's ills.

"Here." She passed the steaming hot mug with a certain reverence. "Drink it well."

Anne Marie thanked her and took a sip. It was sweet and yet salty at the same time, and had an aftertaste.

"What did you do then, dear?"

Anne Marie had to think. The walk home from the alley was a blur. "I don't know. I may have weeded someone's garden, I'm not sure."

Miss Colorado laughed, and in response, so did Anne Marie. "God, I'm weird!"

"No, you're not. You're precious," Miss Colorado said. "Drink some more."

Anne Marie took another sip. "Am I losing my mind?"

Miss Colorado shook her head. "There are people who think I never had one, so I'm really not the person to ask."

Anne Marie smiled.

"But since you did ask...."

Anne Marie settled back.

"It's been my experience that people who question their sanity, as a rule, don't normally have a problem. It's the ones that never give it a thought...."

Anne Marie nodded. Still. "I never know if I'm seeing people for real, or if it's just all in my head."

"All perception is in one's head. It's the key element in magic. Step right up," Miss Colorado said.

Anne Marie laughed, already feeling mellow. "What's in this?"

"Herbs."

"Legal?"

"Quite."

Anne Marie took a larger swallow. "Will you read the leaves?"

"Of course."

Anne Marie blew on what was left to try and cool it faster. "I didn't know the veteran's dad owned the building."

"He bought it specifically so his son could live here," Miss Colorado said.

"He's all right by the way. I checked on him this morning."

"I know. So did I."

Anne Marie took another drink, and then another, and noticed a sudden change come over Miss Colorado. "What? What's the matter?"

"Nothing, dear," she said.

"Please, it's all right. Tell me."

"It's Laura."

"What? You mean my Laura? Laura, Laura?"

Miss Colorado nodded. "Finish your tea, dear. Maybe it'll tell us something."

Anne Marie gulped the rest and handed her the cup. "Here," she said, and felt flushed, lightheaded. "What's it say?"

Miss Colorado stared through her thick glasses, turning and turning the cup, and shook her head, until finally a shape took form. An hour glass. "Time is running out."

"For who? Laura?"

"No. For both of you."

"Bullshit!" Danny said, when Anne Marie told him about it later. "Why do you believe this woman anyway?"

Anne Marie looked at him. "Why would she lie? Besides, I saw it too."

"An hour glass."

Anne Marie nodded.

"An hour glass out of the blue, which for some mysterious reason she associates with you helping this Laura."

Anne Marie nodded again, but not as convincingly. "Why are you being so negative? I thought you believed and that...."

"I do. At least I did. There was something, I admit it, I felt it too. I just think this is a stretch. An hour glass. Does it actually look like an hour glass? Could I see it? Could anyone see it?"

Anne Marie turned away, or at least tried to, but Danny wouldn't let her and pulled her into his arms. "I'm sorry, I don't mean to imply...."

"You're not implying anything, Danny, you're just saying it. You think I'm seeing things, you think she's seeing things. And yet we both saw the same thing. The woman's practically blind, doesn't that mean anything?"

Danny searched her eyes, and with such confusion in his own, Anne Marie shook her head. "I'm sorry. You should've stayed believing."

"I told you, I do believe. I believe in us. I believe in everything that happens between us." He kissed her gently, but with purpose, holding on, to her...to them. "I believe in us, Anne Marie."

Anne Marie swallowed hard. "And the dress?"

He glanced away.

"The voices?"

Danny looked at her.

"The phone ringing? The music?"

Danny gazed into her eyes, and ultimately smiled in surrender. "Don't go to New Orleans."

"What? Why would I go to New Orleans?"

"I don't know. I just think that's where you're headed. I think that's where your neighbor's got you headed."

Anne Marie shook her head. "How? I don't have any money, and I don't have a job. I'm not going anywhere."

"Promise me," he said, kissing her.

"I promise."

CHAPTER THIRTY-SIX

Anne Marie's mother threw up when she entered the room, and then again and again. "Oh, Lord," she kept saying. "Oh, Lord." Her going home today was obviously out of the question. Nor did she feel much like company.

"Go find a job," she told Anne Marie. "Go."

"All right. I'll be back later."

"Don't bother." Her mother waved her hand in that dismissive way of hers, and that set off the IV alarm and annoying beeping. "Damn!"

Anne Marie waited for the nurse to appear, then left. It was cloudy, not a hint of blue sky or sun anywhere. How was she to tell the time? She debated reentering the hospital to look for a clock, but decided against it. She was getting hungry, so she figured it had to be close to noon anyway, her lunchtime for the past two years. She'd better hurry. If she didn't eat soon, she'd cross a line of sorts and wouldn't want anything until dinner; that's how her stomach worked. She headed for her favorite street vendor's.

"Noon, right on the dot," he told her, and she walked along munching a chili dog. They'd finally gotten around to working on the burned buildings. The hardware was bustling and scheduled to reopen this afternoon. Apparently all it needed was mopping up, airing out, and some minor carpentry.

"We were lucky," the owner told her, when she seemed interested. "It had just spread to us when the fire department arrived."

Anne Marie asked about the vintage clothing store.

"Oh, she'll be back. In the meantime though...." The man said she was setting up shop in her home and lived over on Chippewa.

"Well, good for her." Anne Marie spent the rest of the afternoon going from one place to the next, filling out applications, and had two on-the-spot interviews. Both personnel managers all but offered her a position right then and there based on her aptitude test, typing, and experience, but said they had to check her references first, and she wondered....

What would Headlands say about her?

Would it be the truth?

Would she ever work again?

When she returned to the hospital, her mother was feeling much better. "There's a bug going around. The doctor doesn't think it's chemo related at all. And I still have my hair."

Anne Marie smiled.

"Did you find a job?"

Anne Marie's smile faded. "No."

"Did you try?"

"Yes. As a matter of fact, I did. Some are checking my references."

"What references? What do you think the Headlands Employment Agency will say?"

Anne Marie stared. It was one thing for her to wonder, but quite another for her mother. "I don't know and I don't care."

"Right." Her mother looked out the window and heaved a sigh. "It's getting late."

Anne Marie agreed. It was time to leave. "I'll see you tomorrow."

"Anne Marie?"

She turned back from the door.

Her mother hesitated. "I have no savings. I wish I did, but I don't. All I have is the house."

"So. I don't want anything."

"I know. I'm only telling you, just in case...."

"I'll see you tomorrow."

Anne Marie walked and walked forever, past the medical buildings, the offices and the strip malls, the parking garages and the bars. Past the hub, past the bus station, and finally past the zoo. "Thank God." For sometime now, she thought she might be lost, but the zoo she knew well from when she was a child. She wasn't that far from home. At her present pace, she'd be there in an hour easy. Still, she backtracked and waited at the stop for the rapid like a good little girl, along with two other pedestrians she didn't dare talk to, and boarded and paid her fare. As the streets whisked by, she tried to retrace her route but couldn't, and wondered what had happened to her sense of direction? Where did she go wrong? And why wasn't she hungry? It was dinner time.

Her lack of appetite transformed itself about ten minutes after she arrived at her apartment. She ate everything she could get her hands on. Back and forth to the kitchen she went, past the dress each time, and eventually noticed the cactus.

"Oh my God!" Milt said wait a while to water it, that even though theoretically it was due several days ago, to leave it be. "Now look at it." It was withering. And not a little, a lot.

She phoned him. "Do I water it or what?"

"Is the soil moist?"

"Wait, I'll go check." Anne Marie hurried into the living room and back. "Yes."

"As moist as the other day?"

"Just about."

"Then it's not water."

Anne Marie sat down on the tub. "What is it then?"

"Well, without seeing it to be sure, I'd have to say it sounds like...."

"No, wait." She didn't want to hear it. "I'll bring it in tomorrow. Will you be there?"

"Of course."

"Good, I'll see you then." Anne Marie hung up and went back in and sat down next to it. "What's the matter with you?" she asked, as lovingly as if she were talking to a family pet. "What's wrong?" It seemed to be withering more and more right before her very eyes. "Is it this place? Don't you like it here?" She looked around. "Everything's the same almost. Look. The couch, the chair." Everything except for the dress.

The dress.

She got up, took it by the hanger and headed into the bedroom, but changed her mind and hung it on the back of the bathroom door instead. "There. Now behave," she told it, and laughed. She sounded like her mother.

Danny had to work late, so she wasn't expecting him and was surprised when he knocked on her door. "How long can you stay?"

"I can't. I just stopped by to say hi," he said, kissing her. "I missed you."

Anne Marie smiled. She missed him too.

"I have to pull another double tomorrow, but what about Wednesday. You want to do something?"

"Sure."

Danny smiled and kissed her good-bye. "I'll call you if I get a chance. How's your mom?"

Anne Marie shrugged.

"I'll see you Wednesday."

Alone...again, and with it too quiet, Anne Marie put on the Golden Oldies CD, ran her bath water, and left the door open so she could hear the songs. Judy phoned right after she got in the tub, and they talked for a while. She hung up and washed her hair, and had just gone completely underwater to rinse it when she heard a loud bang. She surfaced with a splash, looked out the door through the water in her eyes, and gasped. The plant had tipped over.

"Oh my God!"

The CD had stopped too.

She froze, staring...waiting for it to start up again, but there was only silence. No music, no noise from the other apartments, no sounds of distant traffic. Nothing. She glanced at the door, too far to close from where she sat, and got out quickly, dried, and dressed. Tiptoeing barefoot into the living room, she looked around. The lamp was off. What? She glanced into the kitchen. The clock was stopped. The refrigerator quiet. She noticed the bathroom light out as well then, and with that, sighed. The power was out. That's all. The bang was probably a transformer somewhere. Nothing to panic about. But then again, that didn't explain how the cactus fell.

She set it gently upright, fussing over it, being ever so careful, and at that point noticed something. The yarn she'd used to secure the splint had been untied. Not frayed or cut or worn, untied. She quickly repaired the splint and patted down the dirt, all the while wondering who could have done this and why. And not knowing where else to turn, she went across the hall to Miss Colorado's, whose apartment was lit with dozens and dozens of votive candles. It seemed she was expecting her.

"How nice. I just made us tea."

Anne Marie stared in awe.

"Come in, dear. Please. Come in."

CHAPTER THIRTY-SEVEN

Anne Marie set out bright and early in search of an abandoned shopping cart for the cactus, but came up empty-handed and out of time. Why, she wondered, when she wasn't looking for one, were they everywhere? Obviously the supermarket parking lots had plenty, but borrowing one of those would be a different thing. She'd have to try looking again later.

Her mother was sitting in a chair for today's chemo, progress, and had yet another roommate, an elderly woman who seemed obsessed with her call button. "Do you see it?"

"I believe it's in your hand," Anne Marie said politely.

"Where?"

"In your hand." Anne Marie showed her. "Right here, see?"

"She's from a home," her mother whispered. "She says they hide it from her there."

"Would you get me some water, nurse?" the woman asked.

Anne Marie looked at her mom. "Is she allowed water?"

Her mother nodded.

Anne Marie poured ice water into a plastic cup from a container on the woman's table.

"Get her a straw."

Anne Marie glanced around. "Where?"

"There's some in my dresser." Rebecca pointed gingerly, refusing to set off the IV.

Anne Marie opened her mother's top drawer and smiled at her stash. Sugar, straws, salt and pepper, artificial sweeteners.... She could open a black market.

"Be careful," Rebecca cautioned, as if Anne Marie weren't nervous enough, with the old woman trembling and trying to gulp down every last drop.

"Do you want more?"

"No. Thank you." The woman licked her thin, frail lips and seemed momentarily satisfied. But then.... "Do you see my call button?"

"It's right here."

Anne Marie left the hospital later, headed for Chippewa. If the vintage storeowner had set up shop at home, there was a chance she might have an old shopping cart. Of course she'd have to find this house first and Chippewa did run city-wide, though she got the distinct impression from the man at the hardware that it was somewhere right around the corner, and basically this was a neighborhood where most of the business owners were still local, so....

She got lucky. Not only was there a sign out front, the woman was standing on her porch accepting a bag of donated clothing, and recognized her. "You were right," she said. "Look at this place." She stood back for Anne Marie to see into her living room, which had become a crowded warehouse of boxes and assorted bags. "The spare bedroom's filled too."

Anne Marie smiled. The woman looked exhausted, but in a satisfied, happy kind of way. "When do you think you'll be back in your store?"

The woman wiped her brow. "Well, they say two weeks, but I'm hoping sooner. At this rate, I'll be sleeping out in the garage by then."

Anne Marie laughed. "You wouldn't happen to have an old shopping cart, would you?"

The woman shook her head. "No, just a come-along."

"You mean a wagon?"

"No." She motioned for Anne Marie to follow her. "Here," she said, pointing to a rather ancient, rusty cart on two wheels hidden under a mound of dresses on hangers. "It was somebody's grandmother's."

Anne Marie smiled. It was perfect, that is if the wheels worked. "Do you mind...?"

The woman shook her head and sat down to take a breather as Anne Marie peeled off the layers and examined it. One wheel turned, the other didn't.

"Maybe it just needs oil."

"Maybe." Anne Marie tried it again. "How much would you sell it for?"

"Nothing." The woman lit a cigarette. "Take it."

Anne Marie stiffened. "No, really I...."

"I'm serious, take it. I don't have a license to sell anything here anyway. We're zoned residential. I'm only allowed to accept donations on the premises."

"Then think of this as a donation," Anne Marie said, digging into her pocket for some money.

"Sorry, no can do." The woman took a long drag off her cigarette. "You either take it for nothing or not at all. Come on, look at it. At best, it's a piece of shit."

Anne Marie laughed. But even so. "Can I trade you something?"

"I don't know. What'd you have?"

"Time," Anne Marie said. "I'm presently unemployed."

"No kidding. You, the guardian angel that you are."

Anne Marie blushed. "I'm not an angel." A witch maybe, according to her mother over the years. But an angel, no.

"Listen, sweetie, you don't know what you did for me that day. I'd lost all hope."

Anne Marie looked the other way. "How about if I help you sort for a couple of hours in exchange for...."

"All right, fine."

She didn't have to ask twice.

The woman smiled and motioned to a mountain of battered boxes in the corner. "If anything's stained or torn or has buttons missing, they go over there. Otherwise." She snuffed her cigarette out. "They go over here. Okay?"

Anne Marie nodded, went to work, and was soon carting her come-along home, rickety-wobbly on one wheel and screeching. She didn't have any oil, she didn't think she did. Vaseline would have to do, she decided, and gooped it on both axles. Halfway to the nursery, with the cactus snug in its tight fit, both wheels started turning, and pulling it became a breeze. A pleasure.

Milt ruined her good mood.

"What do you mean it's dying?"

"I'm sorry."

"Wait a minute." Anne Marie sat down. "Are you saying it looks worse than it did the other day?"

Milt nodded, though not unsympathetically.

"How?"

"I don't know, you tell me. Did you water it?"

"No."

"Well, somebody did."

"It wasn't me."

Milt crossed his arms and sighed. Semantics.

"I don't understand. I talked to it, I gave it sun, I left it alone."

"How alone?"

Anne Marie stared, a thought crossing her mind then, one she tried hard to suppress. "Could it uh...be tears maybe?"

"Tears?" Milt frowned. "You mean like seeping?"

Anne Marie nodded. "Something like that."

"I don't know, I'm not sure." He studied the cactus from every angle.

"You did say it was in shock," she reminded him, desperately needing an explanation. There had been only two people in the apartment lately, she and Danny. And Danny wouldn't water it, not after she told him not to and why. Why would he?

"I guess anything's possible."

"All right. If so, what do we do now?"

"Honestly?"

"Yes."

Milt hesitated. "I say we bury it."

"What?"

"Bury it. Up to here," he clarified. "We need more soil to absorb the moisture."

Anne Marie let out a sigh of relief. She'd thought....

"And quickly," Milt added. Because right before their eyes, as if to erase all doubt, the cactus started to weep. A little at first, tiny droplets from where it had been hurt. Then everywhere.

CHAPTER THIRTY-EIGHT

Angela's Fashions, according to the woman who answered the phone, was a specialty shop and had been in business for sixty years. Working alone in the store at the moment and extremely busy with customers, she said she would be happy to send Anne Marie a flyer, took her name and address, and that was that.

Anne Marie made herself a peanut butter sandwich and phoned the two companies from yesterday's job-hunting efforts. Thank them for the interview, she'd heard the personnel counselors at Headlands say time and time again to their applicants. Tell them how very much you'd like to work for them, say something nice about the company, be eager but not pushy, and ask them if....

Both men cut her short. She was no longer being considered.

"We're still looking."

"The position has been filled."

"Good day."

Anne Marie hung up and stared at the wall. She'd been so sure.

The phone rang.

"Anne Marie?"

It was her mother. "Is that you? You sound funny."

Anne Marie cleared her throat.

"I'm being discharged. Can you come drive me home?"

Anne Marie glanced at her wrist for the watch that wasn't there.

"The keys to the car are at the back door."

The keys to the car were always at the back door. "What time?"

"Eight."

"Eight?" In the evening? That seemed odd to Anne Marie.

"Why? This isn't a hotel. Everybody doesn't have to be out by morning. Are you coming?"

"Yes. I'll be there." She hung up, found her purse, and examined her driver's license. Still valid. She had another two months. What if she got in the car and just kept driving?

Her mother was sitting in the chair, waiting. "Thank heaven. You're late."

It was twenty after. "Sorry." Anne Marie looked around. Her mother had everything packed and ready. "Where's your roommate?"

"She died."

"What?" Anne Marie's mouth dropped. The woman seemed fine this morning. Old obviously, very old in fact. But fine. "When?"

Her mother rang for the nurse. "A little after two. She died in her sleep. I knew the moment it happened."

"How? What do you mean?"

"She stopped breathing, Anne Marie. That's what happens when people die."

Anne Marie shook her head. Talking to her mother was such fun. "Are you ready?"

Her mother gave her a look. "I have to wait for transport. From what I understand, they're running behind."

"I see." Anne Marie sat down and stared at the old woman's bed, made up like a soldier's. Blankets pulled tight, corners tucked under. She pictured her marching. To heaven maybe. "Onward Christian soldiers, marching as to...."

"Anne Marie."

She turned.

"She said you were a sweet girl. She made a point of telling me that."

Anne Marie studied her mother's expression, wondering if she'd rolled her eyes in response, and set the woman straight. "Do you know who she reminded me of?"

"Who?"

"Auntie May."

Rebecca smiled, nodding to herself as if she agreed, and saddened. Auntie May was her favorite. "The room darkened when she died."

Anne Marie stared, for once knowing better than to ask for clarification. Auntie May or the old woman? Back then or now? She just listened, and watched, as a myriad of colors swirled round and round her mother's face. Lovely shades, her grandmother would say. Then none. "Go see what's keeping the nurse. I've had enough of this place."

CHAPTER THIRTY-NINE

Every star in the universe was shining, but no moon. Anne Marie looked for it everywhere. It was odd, eerie. Not a night for walking, she decided, and rode the bus. As she arrived home and entered her apartment, the phone was ringing. It was Danny.

"Where have you been? I've been trying you for hours."

"At the hospital, why?"

"I got off early and was hoping we could do something. I thought about just coming over, but I was afraid if you weren't home I might end up sitting out in the hall with company."

Anne Marie stared. Why the reference to Jimmie? And why the sarcasm?

"Where'd you go?"

"To my mother's." She sat down on the edge of the tub and found herself checking behind the door to make sure the dress was still there. "Someone untied the cactus."

"What?"

"The cactus. Someone untied it."

"You mean the splint?" Danny asked, obviously irritated with her changing the subject.

"Yes. And the power was out."

"Today?"

"No, last night."

Danny sighed. "So who all have you had over?"

"No one. Except you."

"Me? What are you saying?"

"Nothing."

"You think I did it?"

"I didn't say that."

"You might as well have."

Silence.

"All right. I'll see you around." Click.

Anne Marie put down the receiver and just sat there. I'll see you around? That's good-bye. He was telling her good-bye. Adios, just like her mother said. "I'll see you around."

She stared at the floor. If *he* didn't untie the cactus, then who did? She glanced into the living room. It could be anyone, with all the people she had hanging outside her door lately. What made her think it was Danny?

I didn't. I don't. I'm paranoid.

"You don't trust anyone," Jimmie used to say, when he was cheating all along. "You don't even trust your own mother."

"That's unfair."

"No, it's not. It's the truth."

The phone rang.

"No." She refused to answer it and ran her bath water instead. If I don't answer it, then whoever it is won't be able to hang up on me.

"Anne Marie?"

She heard a distinct voice between rings.

"Answer it."

"But Grandmother...."

"Answer it."

She slipped off her shoes and tested the water. It wasn't often she disobeyed her grandmother, particularly not since her death.

"When you were a child though...."

Anne Marie smiled. Obstinate, she used to call her. Obstinate as hell.

"Answer it."

Anne Marie picked up the phone. "Hello."

"I'm sorry," Danny said. "I didn't mean to...."

Neither did she. "Me too. I didn't think you untied the cactus. I don't know why I said that."

"Can I come over?"

"Why?" Anne Marie asked, wanting him to say....

"To be with you."

"To be with me?"

Danny's voice softened. "To make love to you, Anne Marie. I want to make love to you, again and again and again."

Anne Marie started slowly peeling off her clothes. "I don't know. I was just now going to take a bath, and it's awfully late...."

"Unlock your door," Danny said.

Anne Marie glanced into the living room and slid her panties down her legs. "I'm not dressed," she said.

Danny drew a quickened breath. "I don't live that far away. I'll only be about ten minutes. Unlock your door," he said, "and don't get dressed."

Anne Marie smiled. "Hurry."

"I'll be right there."

Anne Marie hung up and tiptoed into the living room, where for a second she almost changed her mind, but for the fire inside. His voice was the only one she could hear, ten minutes an eternity as she immersed herself in the water and until she felt his hands, felt herself being lifted, and felt herself going higher and higher. And higher.

"I can fly, Danny," she whispered against his wet skin. "I can't believe it. I can fly."

CHAPTER FORTY

Anne Marie heard a faint knock from somewhere and rolled over and stretched in bed. Naked, was her first thought. I've been naked for at least twelve hours, depending on the sun, and I'm never going to get dressed again. She squinted and glanced out the window.

"Anne Marie?" She heard the knock again.

"Oh no." It had to be at least noon. "Coming! I'll be right there!" She threw on her robe, combed her fingers through her hair, and hurried to answer the door.

"Hi!"

Miss Colorado peered up at her. "I have tea for your mother. Just what the doctor ordered."

Anne Marie yawned. She'd wrapped the tea in a swatch of muslin and had tied a pink ribbon around it. Oh, would her mother love this. "Thank you."

"Tell her only a little at first. Drink it weak, then stronger and stronger. Let me know if she needs more."

"I will." Anne Marie thanked her again. "This is so nice of you."

"Nonsense," Miss Colorado turned to leave, and hesitated. "I had a dream last night, a vision."

Anne Marie smiled, hoping that somehow in her dreams she was able to see everything perfectly clear. "Who was it about?"

"Why you, dear, of course."

"Me?" And why, of course?

"I'll tell you all about it later. I'm expecting a call."

Anne Marie's mother balked at the tea, as Anne Marie feared she would. "How do we know what's in it?"

"We don't."

"How do we know it's not poison?"

Anne Marie sighed. "Why would she poison you, Mom? She doesn't even know you."

Her mother looked at her. "What's that supposed to mean?"

Anne Marie shook her head and laughed. "Nothing. Come on, I'll have some with you."

Her mother watched Anne Marie pour both cups, and when served, crossed her arms and stared out the window. "Why don't we go dig up the camera?"

Anne Marie sat down. "Why don't we have a cup of tea first."

Her mother rolled her eyes. "You and that goddamned tea."

Anne Marie laughed. Nothing was going to ruin her mood today. Not her mom, not Miss Colorado's dream, not being unemployed, nothing.

"Are you saying you don't want to dig up the camera?"

"Not today, no. I've got to go find a job, remember." It was already three, and Danny was coming over at seven. "We'll dig it up when I come over tomorrow."

"You don't have to come every day."

"I know. Now come on, taste your tea." Anne Marie sipped her own and licked her lips. "It's good."

"Hmph." Her mother blew on the cup, reluctantly took a drink, and admitted it wasn't bad, but wouldn't let up. "What if it interferes with my medication?"

"It won't."

"How do you know?"

Anne Marie shrugged. "I just do. She knows what's she doing."

"Right."

Anne Marie drank the rest of hers, rinsed out her cup and put it in the strainer, and said she had to leave. "Do you need something from the store or anything?"

Her mother shook her head. "Sophie went shopping for me."

Anne Marie nodded, figuring as much. Someone had come in and straightened up and made her mother's bed as well. "Okay then, I'll see you tomorrow."

Anne Marie walked to the corner and boarded when the bus pulled up and stopped, in case her mother was watching from the front window. "Can I have my money back?" she asked the driver a block later, saying she'd changed her mind.

"Sorry," he said, and motioned to the lock on the box.

"Wonderful." Anne Marie frowned and sat back down. She might as well ride.

Judy was sitting on the stoop having a beer with the veteran when Anne Marie returned home. "Hey, how's it going?" the man said, his usual greeting and offering her a beer as well.

"Thank you." Anne Marie removed the cap and took a long drink. "What are you doing here?" she asked Judy.

"I want my fortune read."

"What?"

"I want to meet your neighbor. Your other neighbor I mean," she said, smiling as she glanced at the veteran. "When you weren't home I was going to leave, but John here said you were due home, so...."

Anne Marie looked at the veteran. John. Due home?

"I had a hunch," he said, grinning.

Anne Marie shook her head and turned to Judy. "Why do you want your fortune read? She's not a fortune teller."

"That's not what your mom said."

"My mom?"

"I stopped by right after you left I guess. She told me all about her and we had tea. Where have you been?"

Anne Marie sat down and sighed. "I went to the bus station."

"The bus station? Why? What for?"

"To fill out an application. The bus driver said they were hiring."

Judy downed the rest of her beer. "I can't believe you haven't found a job yet, you're so...."

Anne Marie gave her a look, only now realizing they probably shouldn't be discussing this in front of the veteran, not with his dad owning the building. "Come on." When she motioned for Judy to follow her, the veteran leaned back out of the way.

"See ya," he said, saluting them with his beer bottle.

"You too." Anne Marie thanked him again for the beer and smiled. John. He looked like a John. Big bad John, she thought. And in a flash, the air turned hot and sticky and she saw him in uniform, his face smeared and dripping. And mud, and tar, and blood. All over his hands.

He looked at her, guilty, with tears way back in his eyes, and Judy tugged at her arm.

"Come on," she said, and the veteran smiled.

"I'm sorry," he whispered. "I'm so sorry."

Anne Marie nodded. "I know." She touched his arm and then his face. "I know."

CHAPTER FORTY-ONE

Miss Colorado must have known, Anne Marie decided. Why else would she answer the door dressed the part? "How much do you charge?" Judy asked, wide eyed and enthralled with her Madam Guru getup.

"That all depends," Miss Colorado said. "If I see great wealth in your future, I up the fee."

Anne Marie laughed. "And if you don't?"

"Then it's free. Come in, come in."

Judy looked around. "Oh my God," she muttered, entering on Anne Marie's heels. "Can you believe this?"

Anne Marie nudged her with her elbow, a way of warning her yet again to mind what she said. No stupid questions and no stupid remarks. In and out, was the way Anne Marie wanted this to go; Danny was due in less than an hour.

Miss Colorado motioned for Judy to sit down, and donning her glasses, studied her face up close. "Cards, tea leaves, or palm? What's your pleasure?"

Judy hesitated, obviously taken aback by the vastness of her magnified eyes. "Uh...."

"Her palm," Anne Marie answered for her, hoping to move this along. "She has nice hands."

Miss Colorado agreed. "Well now, let me see...."

Anne Marie's mind wandered. "Good health," she heard. "Long life. Kind heart." All the usual sort of things her grandmother used to start with. She looked at a painting on the wall. It was of a lioness and a cub; the lioness with her paw stretched over the cub's back and the cub intent on something far off in the distance.

"True love."

Anne Marie turned.

"This man has always been true to you and loves you dearly, though he has hurt you many times."

"Loves her dearly?"

Judy was smiling from ear to ear, and with tears in her eyes. "Honestly, you can see that?"

"Yes."

"Will we get married?"

Anne Marie shook her head. She hoped not. Phil was trouble. He always was, and always would be.

"Yes."

"Yes?!" Judy squealed. "We will?"

Miss Colorado nodded.

"Wait a minute." Anne Marie started to say something, but from the look on Miss Colorado's face, thought better. "Sorry."

Miss Colorado nodded and turned her attention back to Judy. "I see problems."

"Problems?"

"With a friend."

Anne Marie sat back. This was unfair. Her grandmother used to do this kind of thing too.

"You and this friend will have to resolve your differences, or it will cause nothing but pain for both of you."

"Oh yeah?" Anne Marie said. "Well, what if he's an asshole?"

Miss Colorado looked at her, and with enormous effort not to laugh. "He is not. And if he is, he will outgrow it."

Anne Marie shook her head.

"Is there more?" Judy asked. "Will we have children?"

"Yes." Miss Colorado furrowed her sagely little brow. "I see three, no, four children. Three boys and a girl."

Anne Marie rolled her eyes. Phil, a father of four; what a scary thought. And just about the time she figured the reading had come to an end, Miss Colorado started up again about the supposed trouble with a friend. Trouble that could be avoided.

"All right, all right," Anne Marie said to herself. "You made your point. Let's not overdo it."

"We wouldn't want a recurrence of last summer," Miss Colorado cautioned.

What? What, last summer, Anne Marie wanted to know. She looked at Judy, who for some reason lost all color and expression.

"Do not attempt that again."

Attempt what? Anne Marie glanced from one to the other. And with that, the reading was over. Miss Colorado served tea.

"What's she talking about?" Anne Marie whispered, when she'd gone back into the kitchen for a plate of cookies.

Judy cleared her throat and shrugged. "I don't know."

"You do too. Tell me."

Judy shook her head. "I told you, I don't know."

"Then ask her. Ask her to explain. Don't you want to know?"

Judy shook her head. "It won't happen again, so forget it. Didn't you hear her?"

Anne Marie sat back and nodded. She'd heard her. And after this, would not doubt the woman again. Because whatever had showed up in Judy's palm.... She reached for it to see for herself.

"Anne Marie?" Miss Colorado said.

She raised her eyes.

"Your telephone man is here."

Anne Marie turned, and just then heard a knock on her door across the hall.

"He has flowers for you."

"What?"

"Roses."

Anne Marie smiled. She was playing with her now, getting back at her for doubting. "Really? What color?"

"Red," she said.

And red they were.

CHAPTER FORTY-TWO

Judy was on cloud nine. Not only did she just have the best reading in the world, she got to meet Danny, the infamous telephone man. "I'm going to be getting married," she told him.

"Really," he said, making polite conversation. "When?"

"I don't know. Phil hasn't asked me yet."

Danny turned. What was there to say? He motioned to the door, and Anne Marie nodded yes. Miss Colorado had told her.

"We'll see you guys Saturday," Judy said, having insisted the four of them all go out and get acquainted. She hugged Anne Marie. "I'll call you tomorrow."

Anne Marie closed the door and groaned.

"What's the matter?" Danny asked.

She shook her head. "You'll see. He's a jerk."

Danny smiled and, watching Anne Marie arrange the roses in the goldfish bowl, found himself smiling again. "So where do you want to go?"

Anne Marie said she was depressed and didn't want to go anywhere at first, but then changed her mind and voted to go to the fifties diner. Once there, she leafed through the jukebox selections and made a discovery. "Look!"

"What?" Danny laughed.

"It's that 'Big Blue Diamond' song."

"So." Danny dug into his pocket for some change and played it. "What's the big deal?"

"It's the song the vintage shop owner wanted to know about. I couldn't remember it the other day, but now I do." She knew every word by heart. "How could I forget?"

Danny shrugged. How could she remember? "Did your mom used to play this kind of music?"

"I don't think so. No. Why?"

"It was just a thought."

Anne Marie smiled. "Maybe I was a disc jockey in a previous life."

Danny selected two more tunes at random, and marveled when she knew all the words to these as well. "This is weird, really weird."

"I know."

She couldn't wait to tell the vintage shop owner, and on the way to her mother's the following day, stopped by her house. "You're kidding. You mean, it was Little Willie John?"

Anne Marie nodded, and sang her the chorus, just to be sure. "Is that the one?"

"Yes!" The woman all but jumped up and down. "God, that's been bugging me! I don't know how to thank you! Do you want a job?"

"What? Researching old songs?"

"No." The woman laughed. "Helping me here. I'm buried."

Anne Marie looked around. "You mean until you get back into the store?"

"For starters, yeah. Who knows after that?"

Anne Marie glanced around again and gave it some thought. "When do you want me to start?"

"I don't know. Today. Now. Can you start now?"

Anne Marie nodded. "I have to go to my mother's first though. She just got out of the hospital and...."

"That's all right, no problem," the woman said. "Just come back when you can. I'm flexible."

Anne Marie couldn't believe her good fortune. "Do you want me to fill out an application, or do you want references or anything?"

"No. I've seen you work. That's enough for me."

Anne Marie smiled and thanked her. "I'll be back in a little while," she said, and left all excited.

Her mother wasn't so thrilled. "Couldn't you have gotten a real job?"

Anne Marie sighed. "As opposed to a fake one?"

Her mother crossed her arms. "You know what I mean. What kind of job is sorting old clothes?"

"I don't know. What kind of job is...."

"How much does it pay?"

Anne Marie stared and had to think. "I don't know, I didn't ask."
Her mother shook her head.

"Do you want some cottage cheese?" Anne Marie headed for the refrigerator.

"No, I can get it myself. I wouldn't want to keep you from your wonderful new job. Go on. Go."

Anne Marie looked at her. They'd been here before, many, many times. Say something nice, she imagined her grandmother saying. Say something nice.

Not today. Not now. "I'll see you."

"Wait a minute," her mother called after her. "Are you coming tomorrow?"

Anne Marie glared back at her from the screen door. "I thought you didn't want me coming every day?"

"I don't! You're right! Go."

Anne Marie didn't realize how fast she could walk, angry, was back at the woman's house before she knew it, and had to sit down and catch her breath.

"Are you all right?"

Anne Marie nodded. "Fine. Where do you want me to start?"

The woman scanned the room, studied Anne Marie briefly, and settled on a mile-high pile of old wedding dresses. "There. Pick the best one out for the window and sort the rest by size. If they need cleaned or repaired...."

Anne Marie held up her hand, there was no need to explain everything. She was starting to sound a little like her mother. "I got it."

The woman smiled. "I know that. But what I was going to say was, that if they need repaired, perhaps you can take them with you, and...."

Anne Marie stared. "Me? I don't know how to sew."

The woman chuckled. "No, but your neighbor does."

"My neighbor?"

"Yes. Miss Colorado."

"What?"

"She answered an ad I ran once, and if I only drop off a dress or two at a time, I can usually get them back the following day."

Anne Marie swallowed hard. "I don't understand. Are you telling me...?" She couldn't believe this. This would mean.... "The dress I bought. Do you remember the dress I bought?"

The woman nodded.

"Did Miss Colorado repair it?"

"I think so." The woman nodded again, though rather sheepishly this time, and reached for a cigarette. "As I recall, there was a tear in it, but it was no big deal. In fact, when she was done with it, you couldn't even tell."

Anne Marie shook her head and looked faint. "Wait a minute. Where was the tear?" she asked, and more importantly, "How do you know she's my neighbor?"

CHAPTER FORTY-THREE

Anne Marie sat with the cactus and commiserated. To hear Grandmother Light talk, everything that had gone wrong today was all her own fault. "If you sing before breakfast, you'll cry before supper." How many times had she told her that?

"I'm not crying," Anne Marie said defiantly, fighting back tears. But why would Miss Colorado lie? Why didn't she say she'd seen the dress before? She had to have recognized her own work. The first thing Anne Marie did upon returning home was examine the dress, and sure enough, it *had* been torn and repaired across the bust. Tiny little stitches, perfect in pattern and evenly placed, same color thread as the waistline alteration. Why?

"Go talk to her," her grandmother said. "Ask her to explain."

Anne Marie stared out the window. She should've eaten breakfast before she'd left this morning, even if it would have been just peanut butter again, then that way when she'd started singing....

The phone rang.

What a coincidence. It was Miss Colorado, and still sounding like a friend. "Can you come talk to me, dear? There's something I have to tell you."

Anne Marie shook her head, knowing she should say no, but went anyway, and took the dress with her. No more secrets; no more lies.

When Miss Colorado served tea, for the first time, Anne Marie was reluctant to join her. "I think I'll wait till it cools."

"Very well." Miss Colorado took a sip of her own. "In my dream the other night," she said, gently placing her cup down.

Anne Marie stared, she'd forgotten about that.

"You were walking down a long road."

Anne Marie listened, the prom dress on her lap, and thought cynically, what...toward a bright light?

"Toward a bright light."

Anne Marie rolled her eyes. Rubbish. A circus act.

"Then everything went dark, and all you had...."

Anne Marie stiffened.

"Was a flame in your hand."

"A torch."

"Yes, a torch."

Grandmother Light's torch. The one she always said she'd be passing on to Anne Marie someday. "Then what happened?"

"Nothing. That was it. Do you know what it means?"

Anne Marie hesitated and started to say no, but for some reason told her the truth instead. She explained how her grandmother died suddenly, and how she didn't even know she was ill until two days before her death. How there'd been no time. And how her grandmother seemed afraid then, and that she'd never seen her afraid before.

"Perhaps she held on to it too long," Miss Colorado suggested.

Anne Marie shook her head and absentmindedly poured herself a cup of tea, took a drink and then another, and Miss Colorado smiled.

"I suppose you want to talk to me about the dress."

Anne Marie stared. "How did you know?"

Miss Colorado chuckled. "Don't you have it with you?"

"Yes." Of course. The smell, and the sound. Her keen senses. "It doesn't talk to me anymore."

Miss Colorado nodded and solemnly bowed her head. "I told you time was running out. You're the one that chose to ignore that."

"I didn't. Not really. Does that mean it's gone now? That I'll never know?"

Miss Colorado shrugged. "Perhaps if you pay attention."

Pay attention? How could she, she wondered, with all the voices crowding her head? All the doubts. The confusion.

Miss Colorado raised her distant eyes. "You're angry with me, dear. Why?"

Anne Marie hesitated. Was it about the dress? Or was it about Phil? "I wish you hadn't told Judy that. I know it's what she wanted to hear and I'm not sure what you meant about the rest, but.... You don't know this guy, he's so...."

"I only told her what I saw," Miss Colorado said. And that was all she would say. Anne Marie left without even asking about the initial dress repair, waited for night, and took it with her to the roof.

"Oh God," the not-so-friendly lesbian said, from her stretched out position on the chaise, where she'd apparently been stargazing. "It's you and that stupid dress again."

Anne Marie sighed. She'd hoped to be alone; something Danny didn't quite understand earlier. But so much for that. "I'll come back later."

"Why?" Miss Congeniality sat up, indignant. "Afraid I might come on to you? Hey, you're hardly my type."

Anne Marie boarded the elevator. "Who cares? You're giving off bad vibes," she said, and the woman took offense.

"Yeah, well I'm not exactly having a good day."

"Neither am I," Anne Marie said. "So have fun." When she returned after midnight, the woman was gone.

Anne Marie sat in her vacant chair, smiled at her lingering scent of Jasmine cologne, and laid the dress in her lap. Talk to me, didn't work before, so there was no sense trying that now. Besides, she could still see Danny's face when she told him she'd said that in the first place, and even laughed herself. Nevertheless, there had to be some way to communicate. She obviously had this dress for a reason, whether Miss Colorado had sewn it twice or not.

"Maybe the woman put a spell on it," she could hear her mother saying. "Maybe...." On second thought, that really didn't sound like her mother at all. Her mother didn't believe in spells.

"Listen. Open your eyes and listen," her grandmother said, and she tried. She looked at the stars and she looked at the quarter moon. She yawned and yawned and looked some more. All alone. Just her and the dress. Looking and looking and listening. And before long, she was sound asleep.

CHAPTER FORTY-FOUR

Anne Marie woke to a spider web spun across her eyes, and wiped her face again and again throughout the morning, but couldn't rid herself of the feeling. Rita, the vintage storeowner, looked at her from across the room. "Are you all right?"

Anne Marie stared, wondering what she meant. "I guess, why?"

"You seem nervous. What's the matter?"

Anne Marie shrugged. The woman was nice, but hardly knew her, so how could she make such an observation? "I'm fine, really."

Rita nodded, watched as Anne Marie wiped and wiped her face yet again, and went back to work. "What time did you say you have to leave today?"

Anne Marie had to think. Today was payday at Headlands, they closed at five; it would take her at least an hour to walk there, she would definitely have to walk since she had no money left, she should probably go visit her mother, and....

"Listen, sweetie," Rita said, after waiting for an answer that was not forthcoming. "Tell me to mind my own business if you want, but you don't look so good."

Anne Marie glanced at her and ultimately had to sit down. She didn't feel so good either. It was as if all those old feelings from the dress were back, and then some. "I'll be okay, just let me rest a minute."

"Fine." Rita lit a cigarette. "You're the one pushing yourself, though I don't know why. You're making me nervous, for Christ sake. I'm over here trying to keep up with you, and you're half my age. Give me a break!"

Anne Marie smiled a weary smile and mopped her brow, which was cold and damp, took a minute to gather herself, and got up and started in on the clothes again. Miss Colorado was going to be busy tonight. Anne Marie left for the Headlands with a grocery bag full of dresses to be repaired that got heavier and heavier as she walked along. She wasn't looking forward to this, and would like to have phoned and asked to have her paycheck mailed, but that would mean having to wait another day or two, and that prospect was even grimmer.

She waved to her favorite street vendor.

"Where you been?" he shouted.

"Working," she called back, and smiled. If she were lucky, at this pace, she'd arrive just after the usual Friday mad-dash to the door, and at least wouldn't have to see anyone but her old boss.

The man scowled when he looked up from his desk and saw her standing there. A bad penny. "Yes?"

"My paycheck," Anne Marie said. "I'm here for my paycheck."

The man scowled again and folded his arms. "I believe it's being held."

"What?"

"Held. There's been a few things missing around the office."

"So." There were always a few things missing around the office. What did that have to do with her?

"We need to check out a few theories first. Perhaps by next week."

Next week? Anne Marie shook her head, a wave of fear and anger washing over her. "No."

"No, what?" the man said.

"No. Just plain no. You're not going to do this to me. I want my paycheck," she said, her voice growing lower and lower. "And I want it now. Otherwise...." She pointed to the door. "I'm going down to the police station and I'm going to sign an affidavit, and you're going to give me my paycheck one way or the other. Do you understand me? I want my paycheck, and I want it now."

Danny heard the story that night. "Then what did he do?"

Anne Marie leaned back. "He gave it to me and said good riddance."

Danny laughed. "All right, babe!"

"I think he thought I'd actually do it."

"You mean you were bluffing?" Danny got an even bigger kick out of that.

"I don't know. I don't think I was at the time."

Danny smiled and kissed her. They'd planned to go to a movie, the first movie Anne Marie had been to in years, a comedy which started at eight. But they never made it. Anne Marie woke hours later and looked around the room. There was something wrong, and on such a beautiful night.

"Danny. Danny, listen."

He opened his eyes and rolled over.

It was crying. A baby crying. And close by.

Anne Marie got out of bed and tiptoed to the open window and looked out, but the crying sound seemed to be inside her apartment. "You do hear that, don't you? Tell me you hear that."

Danny nodded, half sleep. "Maybe it's out in the hall," he said, but it wasn't. It surrounded Anne Marie and followed her into the living room, then into the kitchen and into the bathroom, and stopped only when she reached for the prom dress and wrapped it gently in her arms.

Danny shook his head and swallowed hard, watching. "Dear God, Anne Marie...." he said. And she nodded.

"It's Laura."

"I know."

"She needs me."

CHAPTER FORTY-FIVE

Jimmie started showing up again. "Twice this morning, when you were gone," Miss Colorado said. "And he's angry."

Anne Marie stared more and more, the other side looming ever so much closer now. "How do you know?"

"Because he kicked the door."

Anne Marie's mother was in a mood as well. "Look at this! Just look at this!" Fistfuls of her hair were falling out. "Why me? Why? After all this, I thought...."

Anne Marie didn't know what to say. "Where did you bury the camera?"

"What?"

"The camera. Where did you say you buried it?"

Her mother shook her head. "I'm losing my hair and you want to go dig up the camera. Now?"

"Yes," Anne Marie said, and in a hurry. "Wear a babushka."

"What?"

"A babushka."

"No!"

"Fine." Anne Marie marched out the back door. "But I'm going to start at the garage, so if you don't want the whole back yard dug up...."

Her mother took off after her. "Don't you dare."

"All right, then tell me where it's at."

"There, in front." Her mother pointed to the Burning Bush at the corner of the flowerbed and fluffed her remaining hair for the neighbors. "Approach it from the right."

Anne Marie stopped dead. "Why?" That sounded like something her grandmother would say. And judging from the immediate expression on her mother's face, apparently she realized it as well.

"Just do it, okay?" Her mother went for a hand trowel, marked the exact location, then disappeared again, and returned as Anne Marie was unearthing a box wrapped in oilcloth.

"I can't believe you saved this," Anne Marie said, carefully unfolding the cloth. It was the one she always used for making clay projects in middle school; the wizard, and the frog, and the shrew, and…. She looked up, saw her mother had put on a scarf, and held her tongue.

"All the other little girls made such nice things."

Anne Marie shrugged and opened the box.

"Oh look." Her mother sank to her knees beside her and adjusted her scarf. "Everything's still dry and in perfect condition."

It wasn't exactly a time capsule by today's standards. Nor did Anne Marie see any evidence of the fury she'd imagined precipitating her mother's actions that day. The contents were nice and neat and meager. Sad almost.

"Here, see…." There were pictures of the dog, Missy, just like her mother said, and the camera with the film still in it, along with a pendant. "Your grandmother's. Gaudy, isn't it?" And the front page of a Wall Street Journal.

Anne Marie stared at the pictures of Missy, a row of four, obviously taken at one of those dollar photo booths, and shook her head. The dog was looking eagerly into the camera in each one, oblivious to her fate it seemed, except for the last. In this one, she'd lowered her eyes and was cowering.

"She rode with her head in my lap the whole way."

"Where did you...?" Anne Marie handed her the pictures.

"These? Woolworth's," her mother said. "I bought her a hamburger first."

Anne Marie smiled, but on the verge of tears.

"I wanted you to have something to remember her by. Besides," her mother said, handing the pictures back and reaching for the Wall Street Journal. "I figured she had to be tired of cat food."

Anne Marie laughed and wiped her eyes, focusing elsewhere. "Look," she said. "There's one more shot left in the camera."

"Oh no, don't even think about it," her mother insisted, backing up. "I look like a studda bubba."

"No, you don't. Come on. Say cheese."

When her mother put on her sunglasses and posed with her hands over her face, Anne Marie laughed.

"Come on...."

"Forget it. I look terrible."

"No, you don't. You look pretty. You look like a movie star."

"Honest?" Her mother lowered her hand from her face. "You're not just saying that?"

Anne Marie shook her head. "No, honest. Now come on, say cheese."

"Cheese," her mother said, posing for real this time. And Anne Marie snapped the picture.

Vince's Drug Store seemed as good a place as any to drop off the film. He was running a special. "Where you been, little lady?" he asked, counting out pills into a dispenser.

"Oh, here and there," Anne Marie said.

"Really? I think I know the place."

Anne Marie chuckled. This man was always in a good mood, even when giving the rundown on who just died. "Old Mr. Murphy," he said. "In his sleep, God rest his soul. Next."

Anne Marie's aches and pains manifested again as she walked home. First in her legs, then her arms and shoulders, and even in her hands. As she turned the corner on her block, she glanced ahead, and there was her father, talking to the veteran one second and gone the next. She started running.

"Wait!" she shouted. "Don't leave!" She wanted to ask him how all of a sudden he knew where she lived, after a lifetime of being told by her mother that he'd obviously forgotten, 'The no-good son of a bitch.' "Wait!"

The veteran watched her run by and hailed her efforts with a beer. "You're not going to catch him. He ain't there," he said.

She didn't hear him. "Damn it! Wait! You can't do this!"

"Wrong thing to say," the veteran commented. "Wrong thing to say. Trust me, I know."

Anne Marie stopped at the corner to try to catch her breath, gripping her side in pain and looking both ways as she debated which direction to take, and ended up facing the veteran.

He patted the step next to him. "Join me," he said, and when she walked back, he moved over and handed her a beer. "So how's it going?" he asked, the same thing he always asked.

"Okay," she said, her customary reply.

And there they sat.

"You got mail," he said, after a while. His box was next to hers.

Probably a bill, she thought, but then remembered about Angela's Fashions, and knew what lie ahead. 555 Magazine Street. A white house with a wrought iron gate. Two steps up and into a vestibule. It was all so clear. I'm here to pick up my dress.

Anne Marie stared, saw a face, and though she'd promised....

"Danny, I'm sorry."

He took her by the hand.

"I know I said I wouldn't go, but I am. I have to. I'm going to New Orleans."

CHAPTER FORTY-SIX

Judy was as giddy as any new bride-to-be, though Phil still had yet to officially pop the question. "When do you think he will?" she asked Anne Marie, whispering.

"How should I know?" She was busy trying to deal with her own dilemmas at the moment. Could she afford the trip to New Orleans? No. How much would a plane ticket cost? Too much. She'd never been on a plane before, would she get sick? When she got there, what would she do? Take a cab? Bus? What? And where would she stay? She looked at Danny. "Did you say they were closed on Mondays?"

Danny drew a breath and sighed. Though the question seemed out of the blue, he knew exactly what she was referring to, Angela's Fashions. "Can we not talk about this for a while?"

"Fine. But if they *are* open on Mondays...."

"They're not," Danny said. "All right?"

"All right."

Phil returned from the bar with a round of drinks, his treat, and a platter of warm tortillas with salsa and melted cheese. "Eat up, I got wings coming too," he said, taking on the role of the perfect host for some reason and, if Anne Marie weren't mistaken, apparently enjoying himself. "So how'd you come to work for the phone company?" he asked Danny. "Did you have to know someone to get in?"

Anne Marie stared. Once a jerk, always a jerk. What a thing to ask. She sipped her drink, remembering the time....

"Actually, no," she heard Danny say. Her mind wandered, only bits and pieces of his explanation penetrating. Two years of technical school. A counselor who took a liking to him. A Chevy, the same year as his. A stock car race. A letter of recommendation.

"So I was right," Phil said. "You knew someone."

Danny smiled. "In a roundabout way, yeah, I guess."

Phil sat back, satisfied. "Anne Marie got me my job."

"Oh?"

Anne Marie shook her head and looked at Danny. "No, I didn't. It was advertised, and...."

"Come on, Anne Marie, don't lie," Phil said, "it's not like you. I'd have never thought of going for an office job in my life if it weren't for you, and you know it."

Judy nodded along, her smile radiating like sunshine. "He's been promoted already, can you believe it?"

No, Anne Marie thought, but refrained from saying it out loud. "Congratulations."

"Thanks," Phil said. "I owe you. Friends like you don't come along every day. A lot of people turned their back on me in the past cause I fucked up. And I'm not saying I didn't, cause I did. But you've always stuck by me, no matter what, and I appreciate it. We appreciate it."

Anne Marie sat there, dumbfounded. So what if she took the heat the night he wrecked his car, drunk, and she had Judy pull him aside so she could climb behind the wheel herself. So what if she'd cleaned out his and Judy's flat the night he got arrested, for fear the cops would come looking for additional evidence there, and did. So what if she loaned him more money over the years than she could count and had yet to get any of it back. And so what if....

"Thanks."

Anne Marie nodded. What was there to say? "You're welcome."

Danny bought the next round, and after that it was time to leave for the movie. "I can't believe how you two are," Judy said to Anne Marie in the ladies room. "It's like you've been together forever."

Anne Marie looked at her in the mirror. "What do you mean?"

"I don't know." Judy said, grinning. "It's just that it's so cool. You're not nervous around each other or anything, and you really haven't even known each other that long. Did you ask Miss Colorado about him?"

"Yes."

"What'd she say?"

Anne Marie hesitated. "She said he was the one."

"The one what?"

Anne Marie stared at her reflection. "I don't know. She wouldn't tell me. She said I'll know when the time comes."

"What? Oh my God! That is so cool."

Anne Marie shrugged and wasn't so sure. After all, Judy was right, she and Danny hadn't known each other that long. And yet.

"Danny," she said, back at her apartment and all curled up, exhausted in his arms. "If it turns out I'm not who I am, and you're not who you are...."

Danny smiled and kissed her on the forehead. "Then that'll mean I'm cheating on you, babe. Because I love you, whoever you are."

CHAPTER FORTY-SEVEN

Anne Marie put on her robe and bunny slippers, ventured out into the hall, then down the winding back stairs to the alley, and sighed appreciatively upon reaching her destination.

The veteran had a cup of hot coffee waiting for her. "Just the way you like it."

Anne Marie took a sip and smiled at him sitting in the window. "How'd you...?"

"I heard water running," he said, as to how he knew she was awake. "I hear everything at night."

Everything? Anne Marie took another sip of coffee, her cheeks turning a pale shade of blush at the thought of such thin walls.

"Hey, it's okay," he said, as if always reading her mind. "It brings back old memories."

Old? He was a relatively young man. "You mean to tell me...?"

He shrugged. "So how's the new job?"

"All right." She wondered what her new boss Rita was going to say when she asked for time off already. She'd know tomorrow. "Listen...."

"To what?" The veteran looked around.

"To me," she said, and smiled. "I want to tell you something. It's important. You have nothing but gentleness around you. All your colors are warm."

"It's the coffee."

"No." Anne Marie shook her head and touched his heart. "It's you."

Danny was half-awake when she returned. "Where you been?"

"Outside. I had coffee with John."

"John...?" Danny opened both eyes. "John who?"

"The veteran. You know." She crawled into bed next to him. "He makes his own coffee every morning, fresh."

"That's nice," Danny said, about to drift off again. "Did you bring me some?"

"No, I had two. Now shhhh...go to sleep." Anne Marie thought about her mother. Yesterday, when she'd promised to bring Danny by to meet her, it was before she'd decided to go to New Orleans, and she hadn't told her mother about that yet.

"Come for lunch."

"No, I don't want you to fuss."

"Fine." She could see her mother's face. "I guess you just don't want me to meet him."

"That's not true." Not entirely at least.

"All right, I won't fuss. How's that? Just sandwiches, okay?"

It was settled. "Do you want me to bring something? Should I stop at the store?"

"No, I'll go with Sophie. You go on now, I don't want you late for your date."

Her mother did fuss however, and couldn't get enough of Danny. "Tell me all about yourself."

Danny smiled.

"And by the way," she said to Anne Marie, who hardly touched her plate. "Tell your neighbor I need more tea. That stuff is really good."

Miss Colorado appreciated the compliment. "I put in a little something extra to take away the bitterness. She probably would have thought I was trying to poison her otherwise."

Anne Marie smiled. This woman was too, too wise.

"So what are you planning, dear?"

Anne Marie sat back and paused. "I don't know. Flying's so expensive. It's over four hundred dollars round trip."

"And the bus?"

"Two-ten. The problem there is, it's eighteen hours one way, and that'll mean missing at least three days work."

"What if you travel at night? Do they run then?"

Anne Marie nodded. "Yes, but...." She'd promised Danny she wouldn't take the bus at night. He said it wasn't safe, not even for a man. Take my car, he insisted, leave early, and drive during the day.

"But what if it doesn't start?"

Danny took that personally and was quiet a moment. "What about your mother's? Why don't you borrow hers?"

"My mother's?" Anne Marie stiffened. "No thank you."

She'd walk first.

"Now that's an idea," she told Miss Colorado. "I'll walk, just like the song says. 'Walking to New Orleans.'"

Miss Colorado laughed. "Okay, and if you get there before Christmas...."

"Christmas?" Anne Marie said. "Try Mardi Gras."

"Ahhhhh, Mardi Gras." Miss Colorado's clasped her tiny hands together. "I love the Mardi Gras."

"You mean you've been there? To the Mardi Gras?"

"Many times. Didn't I tell you? I was born there."

Anne Marie stared. "In New Orleans?"

"Why yes, dear. I thought you knew. Are you sure I didn't tell you?"

"Positive." Anne Marie felt that familiar sense of doubt about this woman creeping into all her pores. "How long did you live there?"

"Oh, until I was eleven or twelve, I guess. When did I tell you I was sold the first time?"

"I'm not sure," Anne Marie said, trying to recall and hoping if she said.... "Thirteen, I believe."

Miss Colorado looked at her with her distant eyes. "Really?"

"Yes."

"Well, that's strange," Miss Colorado said. "I seem to remember being younger at the time. Oh my."

Anne Marie watched her color brighten and fade, and refused to finish her tea. "I'd better get going."

Miss Colorado nodded, fading more and more. "Come see me before you leave, dear."

Anne Marie said she would, but knew even then she wouldn't, and rather than wait until tomorrow to tell the vintage shop owner she needed a few days off, she decided to walk over and tell her now.

Rita seemed to know already. "No problem," she said. "I told you, I'm flexible. But if you wouldn't mind doing me a favor. When you're in New Orleans. You did say you were going to New Orleans?"

Anne Marie couldn't remember if she had or not.

"Of course you did. What would make me say that otherwise? Anyway...." The woman wanted pralines. "Candied pecans. Oh my God, to die for. Here," she said, and gave Anne Marie a ten-dollar bill. "Did you want your paycheck?"

"No." Anne Marie declined the offer. "I'll only be a few days." She wanted to make sure she had some money to come home to. Besides, they never did discuss what she'd be paid and she didn't want to get into that right now. It was Sunday and the banks weren't open anyway. "I'll see you Wednesday."

She'd made a decision. She was leaving tonight. There was an eleven-fifteen bus and she was going to be on it. When Danny called at eight, as he said he would, to see what she wanted to do tonight, she'd inform him she wanted to spend the time alone and cleanse.

"To do what?"

"To cleanse," she told him. "To get in the right frame of mind."

"You can do it on the bus tomorrow," he said. "You'll have the whole goddamned day to cleanse."

Anne Marie stared at the bathroom floor. There was something in his voice, and not just the anger.

"Anne Marie?"

Silence.

"Anne Marie, I'm sorry, all right? I love you. Okay?"

"Okay."

She had her backpack packed and ready to go. Should she inform the Super, she wondered? No, she told herself, that's not necessary. You'll only be a few days, how silly. What then? Her apartment was clean, everything was in order. What? She went up to roof and felt like howling at the moon, her skin hot and literally crawling.

"Listen," she heard her grandmother say. "Listen...."

She gazed around. It was dusk. Still too bright to see the moon, to feel the moon. She would have to hear the moon.

"Listen...."

Anne Marie drew a deep breath and called on her inner spirit. "Guide me," she said, and thanked the stars for coming out. "It's time to leave."

"Then go."

Anne Marie grew calmer and calmer on the way down, and realized why, another decision. Everyone would be all right without her for a few days, even her mother, but not the cactus. It would be entirely alone, nor could she trust its care to anyone. She'd have to take it with her.

She drew her bath water and immersed herself, rinsed her face again and again, and lingered a moment, then got out and dressed quickly. Hurry, she heard a voice say, before the phone rings or someone knocks on your door. Hurry. She hoisted the cactus up and into the come-along, strapped on her backpack with the prom dress folded safely inside, took one last look around, and set out unnoticed for the bus station.

The street was deserted, empty and ever so still in the twilight, until she reached the corner and glanced back. A small crowd of statues had materialized outside her building. Rigid replicas of Miss Colorado and the veteran. Danny and the two lesbians. The vintage storeowner. Her mother with her hand on her hip and scowling. Jimmie and Judy and Phil, and Missy at their feet. Her high school principal and her old boss. Children and women everywhere. And standing behind them all, her father; his face an angry mass as she turned away.

"Hurry," she repeated over and over to the hum of the buggy wheels. "Hurry!"

CHAPTER FORTY-EIGHT

Anne Marie bought her ticket and sat down in the terminal to wait. The cactus drew attention. "You need to water it," one woman from across the way said. "It's too dry."

Anne Marie thanked her for the advice. "When I get to where I'm going," she replied, yawning.

"Water it, hell." An old man reminding her of Mr. Murphy appeared suddenly. "Throw it away and buy a new one when you get there."

Anne Marie frowned. Mr. Murphy would never have said such a thing. Ever. She stuck her tongue out at him, and the old man looked surprised at first, then laughed. He had a cane, which he waved like a magic wand, and just like that, he disappeared.

"Hey, lady."

Anne Marie opened her eyes.

"You're going to miss your bus." It was the clerk from behind the counter. "Gate seven, that way."

Anne Marie was the ninth of only ten passengers boarding. "You're lucky," the driver said. "Otherwise...." He glanced at the cactus and mumbled something about the baggage compartment.

Anne Marie took an aisle seat and hid the cactus from view. She hadn't thought of this as being a problem, and didn't even begin to relax until they were miles and miles down the road. It was a quiet comfortable ride, her own little corner of the world, constantly moving and ever-changing, until somewhere along the way when it all became the same. Fast food restaurants and gas stations illuminating the night.

She leaned her head back and closed her eyes. Riding a bus was second nature to her; she grew up on a bus so to speak, though never one with a bathroom before. Every time someone walked back and forth, her hand instinctively sought out the cactus. She had to remember where she was, on a bus, the Jackson Avenue bus, no, the Magazine Street bus. Don't get lost. Then a streetcar. St. Charles. Are you leaving or coming home?

Coming home, I think. It's Canal Street then, first the streetcar on Canal, then St. Charles. Stop at church, there's crafts to be made in the basement. Popsicle sticks. Yarn. And paste. Taste it, it tastes good. Where do you go to school? McDonough No. 9. Metarie Elementary. McDonough No. 2. Live Oak Junior High. Where? Live Oak. It's across the street from the orphanage. What orphanage? I don't know. What do you mean you don't know? I don't know.

"Miss?"

Anne Marie wiped the sleep from her eyes.

"You're going to have to move over."

"Why?" She cleared her throat. "Where are we?"

"Memphis."

The bus was packed.

"Please."

Anne Marie moved over quickly, not wanting to draw the driver's attention, and had to sit cross-legged to leave room for the cactus, her backpack in her lap.

Her seat partner was a middle-aged woman decked out in a black and gold sweat suit and hat, and carrying a black and gold banner. "I'm a Saints' fan."

Anne Marie nodded; she could see that.

"I'm going down for the game, we all are. What's wrong with your cactus?"

Anne Marie looked at it and sighed. "I don't know."

"Did you water it? It looks like it needs water."

Anne Marie shook her head, still half-asleep. "The soil's too moist. I can't."

"Hmph." The woman felt for herself. "Why don't you repot it then. Start fresh."

Anne Marie stared. "Maybe I will," she said, and smiled politely. "Do you have the time?"

"All the time in the world." The woman laughed at her own joke. "For the time being at least."

Anne Marie smiled again, and looked out the window.

186

"It's six-thirty."

"Thank you."

The woman told Anne Marie her whole life's history, sparing no detail. "Isn't that right?" she'd say, and someone on the bus would always agree. "Are you a fan?"

"What?"

"A Saints' fan? Are you going to the game?"

Anne Marie shook her head.

"So what are you going for?"

Anne Marie hesitated. "For lunch I think."

The woman laughed. "I don't blame you. They have the best food. I gain five pounds each time I come down. Right, Jay?"

"Right."

Anne Marie had a fleeting memory of a delicatessen across the street from a school, where she bought her lunch every day, cheese and mayonnaise and potato chips on a quarter loaf of French bread, all wrapped in white paper, and a Coca-Cola in a bottle. Hurry, you only have a half hour.

"Where's it at?"

"The school? Off Magazine, I believe."

"Oh, then you're from there?"

"I guess so," Anne Marie said. "I used to swim at Pontchartrain Park too."

"When?"

"I don't know. A long time ago."

"You got that right," the woman said. "It closed down in what, '84?"

"Sometime around there," a voice two seats back said. "You do mean the amusement park?"

"Yes," Anne Marie said, without even having to think. The Laugh in the Dark was her favorite ride. She found herself telling the woman all about it, and smiled at how much she remembered. She didn't know why she'd been so worried. She'd be able to find everything. Even locating Angela's Fashions wouldn't be a problem; she could find it in her sleep. She just had to figure out the reason why.

"Who are the Saints playing?"

"The Rams," the woman said. "And we're gonna kick their butt! Who dat? Who dat? Go Saints!"

When the whole bus cheered and started singing, Anne Marie laughed and was soon singing right along with them. "'Oh when the saints, go marching in, oh when the saints go marching in, how I want to be in that number, when the saints go marching in.'"

CHAPTER FORTY-NINE

Everybody took their bags and Saints' paraphernalia with them when the bus stopped for a breakfast break and then lunch, so basically Anne Marie's obsession with the cactus went unnoticed, though she did draw a stare or two when she'd haul it *and* her backpack down the aisle with her every time she had to use the bathroom.

Don't trust anyone, she heard a voice in her head saying. Remember when you used to swim at Annunciation Park and how no one could wear shoes there or even bring a towel, because someone would always steal them. Remember the water, how cold it was, and how they would drain it every day. How it was a half-hour walk away, and you and Linda Martin and Brenda Breaux would run from one dried-up grass tuft to the next to get there, and how it was always the hottest on the way home.

"Well, good luck, Anne Marie. It was a pleasure meeting you."

"Thank you. You too." Anne Marie waved good-bye from the New Orleans bus terminal to the self-proclaimed, number-one Saints' fan as the woman boarded the charter with all the rest. "I hope you win," she said, and then they were gone.

An incredibly lonely feeling washed over Anne Marie as she stood looking up and down the street. Nothing was the same. Nothing. Don't panic, she told herself. Maybe it's because you're tired. She hadn't been able to even doze the last seven or eight hours, and she hadn't eaten all that much, wanting to save money. Just get to Canal Street and go from there.

She started walking. There were people everywhere. A woman hailing a cab gave her directions. "Canal Street? Two blocks, that way." When she finally found it, she wanted to cry. The only thing even vaguely familiar were the streetcars.

"That'll be a dollar ten."

Anne Marie stared. She didn't have change. The sign said exact change.

"You gettin' on or off, ma'am?"

"Uh." She stepped back. "When does the next car come?"

"Fifteen minutes."

Anne Marie hurried to the newsstand on the corner for change. "Sorry, not unless you buy something." She bought a candy bar, ate it in three bites, hurried back to the stop, and waited and waited and waited. She glanced at the sky, the sun was gone.

When the next streetcar finally came, she boarded, took a seat toward the front, pulled the cactus in next to her, and leaned back against the familiarity of the backpack. Maybe when she got to Magazine Street. Maybe when she saw Angela's Fashions. Maybe she'd remember something again then.

If only she weren't so tired.

She turned and looked over her shoulder. It would be dark in a couple of hours. She'd have to find a place to stay, the closer to Angela's Fashions, the better. She got off the streetcar at Magazine, was grateful when she found it only went one way, and walked five blocks. A hint of recognition as she approached the building encouraged her. She'd definitely been here before, yes. It was different, a lot different than she recalled, but exactly as it was shown in the brochure. On the hopes that someone might be inside, that perhaps they lived upstairs, she opened the wrought iron gate, dutifully latched it behind her, and walked up to the door and knocked.

The hours were posted on a small sign. 9-5 Tuesday thru Saturday. She knocked again. "Hello. Is anyone home?"

Something caught her attention out of the corner of her eye, a drape moving way over in the far window, then a hand, a very frail hand with long thin fingers curling around and then slipping back, and a glimpse of an ancient face.

Anne Marie shuddered.

"Go away," she heard a voice say. "Go away. You're scaring me."

Anne Marie turned and couldn't leave quick enough. But where would she go? She got on the Magazine Street bus, dragging the cactus behind her, and sat way in back, her heart pounding hard against her chest. That woman was either dead or a witch, that's all there was to it.

"Grandmother?"

Silence.

"Grandmother, are you there?"

"Miss?"

Anne Marie stared across the aisle at a bearded man in army fatigues.

"Miss, are you all right?"

"Yes," Anne Marie said. "Thank you."

When the man nodded and turned the other way, Anne Marie hesitated and made sure she called for her grandmother silently this time. It wasn't like her to talk out loud. What was happening to her?

There was no reply, just the whir and whir of the tires and this endless ride to nowhere. At every stop, she wondered if she should get off, but stayed, and suddenly she knew where she was going, where she needed to go. She hauled the cactus and backpack up front to talk to the bus driver.

"How far to Jackson Avenue?" she asked.

"About another mile," he said.

And Jackson Avenue is where she got off.

CHAPTER FIFTY

Anne Marie stood on the corner of Jackson and Magazine and smiled. She was home. Or at least in the general vicinity. She recalled a store nearby, a very small store with shelves stacked to the ceiling, where her family bought milk and soap powder and things on credit. Pay me Friday, the owner would say, chewing his cigar as he recorded the amounts in a little memo pad kept under the cash register. "How many?" He sold the best donuts, fresh every morning, and Sunbeam bread. She could see the little girl on the wrapper. And cigarettes, and gum, and Gold Brick candy bars, and Kotex and sanitary belts and toilet paper and aspirin in little tin cans. And creme soda. And pretzels and pork rinds and bobby pins and Aqua Net.

Anne Marie started walking in the dusk. If she remembered correctly, the store didn't close till nine, and she just might make it in time. She was hungry and dying of thirst.

The store was closed, the windows painted over, the doors boarded up. "Wow," Anne Marie said, and wondered when, how long ago. She remembered a house then, not hers, but one belonging to an old couple who used to sell frozen Popsicles in Dixie Cups for a nickel. A white house on a street just past the big super market, with awnings on the front windows and a fence that went all the way around back, and a narrow walkway. She'd know it anywhere.

It wasn't there. She looked on the next street, and then the one after that, the one that used to flood the most when it rained. Another couple of blocks and she'd be at the river. Surely the Mississippi River was still there. She hoisted her backpack higher and tightened her grip on the cactus cart. It was always a little dangerous beyond this point.

"Don't you be goin' there by yourself, ya hear?"

"Remember that guy that laid down on the railroad tracks?"

"Remember the dogs?"

"Do you remember the funeral? And the ferry?"

The ferry. It came into view first, then the water.

"Hey you."

Anne Marie turned.

"What you doin' down here?"

"I'm going to take a ferry ride," she said to the voice in the dark, and stepped so close to the edge of the pier, the voice stayed away. When the ferry docked, she boarded, the only passenger, and stared at the water and the lights. It was the last shuttle of the night. And quiet, so very quiet.

The streets were crowded when she returned, cars racing here and there, horns honking, radios blaring, people everywhere, on the corners, spilling out of bars. She wondered if they were there before?

"Run, girl," she heard someone say. "Run."

She kept walking. She hadn't been able to find the store and the Popsicle house, but the ferry was still there, so surely she didn't live far from here. She heard sirens then, one distant and another close by, and had a feeling she should scramble along with everyone else, but didn't. She stood at the corner and waited, five minutes, ten, then fifteen, until all the commotion died down, and started walking again. Live Oak wasn't far away. She remembered exactly how to get there, and a half hour later, was staring through the gate.

What a beautiful school, she thought, and wondered why she'd never noticed before. The delicatessen was gone, she figured as much, but made a complete circle of the school anyway, just in case, hoping. And the orphanage was gone as well.

"It was right there," she told herself, and could see it in her mind. This had all been a waste of time. She saw the school, saw the neighborhood where she used to live, where someone used to live, maybe Laura, saw the river and rode the ferry, and all this for what? For nothing. She was tired. She was hungry. She was empty. It was completely dark now, and she was scared.

She walked until she couldn't walk anymore, and sat down on the curb and cried. She cried for Laura. She cried for herself. She cried for everyone. "I'm sorry," she said. "I've let you down." The old woman at Angela's Fashions had said go away, and she was right.

She should. She wasn't helping anyone. She wiped her eyes and wiped them again, and took off her backpack to look at her bus ticket. Maybe if she were lucky, she could get back to the station in time to switch her ride to tonight. There was no reason for her to stay. There was no reason for her to come in the first place. This had all been a dream. A nightmare.

"Hey, lady!"

Anne Marie turned, saw a blur as it advanced toward her, and was hit in the side of the head.

"Grab her bag!" she heard someone yell from what seemed like far away. Then another blow!

"No!" she screamed, her voice blasting the night. "No!" She struggled to her feet, horrified as two young men ripped her backpack from her hands and started running.

"Stop! Come back!"

"Fuck you, bitch!" the one shouted, and they vanished in the night.

"Oh my God!" she gasped. She was bleeding. She could feel it running down the side of her face, and could hardly move her right arm for the pain. But more devastating still, was the cactus. She fell to her knees and hovered over it as it lay sprawled on the sidewalk, dirt everywhere, and broken completely in half.

CHAPTER FIFTY-ONE

Anne Marie picked up the cactus and painstakingly scraped up the dirt and put it back. But there was nothing she could do with the severed half of the plant. She couldn't even hold it to her breast to comfort it, which is what she wanted to do, to sympathize with it and tell it how sorry she was. How could she let something like this happen?

She took off her jacket and wrapped it gently inside like a baby, and set it in the cart next to the base. If she only knew where to go, someplace quiet where she could think. What had Milt said? What should she do at this stage? She started walking, the wheels on the cart wobbly and screeching again and difficult to pull. She turned it around and tried pushing it, but that didn't work, so she went back to dragging it, and wiped the blood off the side of her face with her sleeve.

Off in the distance, she heard the stop and start of a bus, and checked her pockets to see how much money she had. Two five-dollar bills and thirty cents in the one, and a ten-dollar bill which was the vintage shop owner's and four singles in the other. She searched the stars for direction, and headed north. Moments later, a passing car slowed to a stop, backed up, and started creeping along next to her.

"Hey you! Hey!" one of the passengers called out the window. "You wanna have a good time?"

"No thank you," Anne Marie said, focusing straight ahead. "I've already had one."

Laughter emanated from the car. "Come on. We'll just take you for a little ride."

Anne Marie glared in their direction at the sound of the door opening, and raised her injured arm effortlessly in warning. "Go away, I said. Leave me alone."

The man stared, mouth open, and slipped back into the car. "Let's go," he told his friends. "Somebody beat her up. Let's go before they blame it on us."

The car sped away, its wheels squealing, and Anne Marie walked on. When she turned the corner, she glanced ahead in the night and felt her heart stop. There was something lying on the sidewalk, something familiar at second glance. She picked up her pace. It was her backpack.

The kids had obviously discarded it, but not before they tore through all its contents and scattered them in the street. Her change of clothes, her bus ticket, her toiletries, they'd emptied her shampoo and toothpaste, apparently used her toothbrush to smear the mess everywhere, and judging from the smell, urinated all over everything on top of that.

She wondered, when they'd found her hotel money, why they didn't just leave the rest alone? Was this a show of anger at there being so little, or their idea of fun? Her insurance card and driver's license were gone as well. What could they possibly want with them? She picked up the prom dress and stood shaking her head. Laura didn't deserve this, not after all she'd been through. She just plain didn't deserve this.

Anne Marie walked to the nearest house, knocked on the door, and when no one answered, went around the side to use the hose, and dumped her trash in the garbage can. Thank you, she wrote on a dollar bill she left stuffed in the handle on the lid for the owner, I hope this covers the cost.

She left a steady trail of water behind her that after a block or two eventually turned into a trickle, and was no longer dripping by the time she boarded the bus. "I'll stand," she told the driver, "if you don't mind."

He shook his head and every so often looked at her in his rear-view mirror. She rode to the end of the line, and paid him another dollar-ten, stood again for this ride, and sat down for the third.

"Hey look, lady," he said. "It's none of my business, but I think you need to go to a hospital."

Anne Marie looked at him. "Why? I'm fine."

The man glanced at the wound on the side of her head, and then at the bundle in her cart.

"I'm just a little lost," she said. "When I recognize where I'm going, I'll get off."

The man nodded, and drew a deep breath and sighed. For the last two runs, it had been just the two of them on the bus. "Listen," he said. "I'm sorry. But I really can't let you keep doing this."

Anne Marie squared her shoulders.

"I know where you can go, where no one'll hurt you."

Anne Marie eyed him suspiciously, pulled the cactus in closer.

"We're not all bad, you know. Some of us are okay," he said, referring to men in general.

Anne Marie stared ahead and out the window right as he said that, and saw her father waiting at the next stop.

"Don't!" she said, when the bus started slowing down. "He's not one of you."

The driver looked at her. "Ma'am?"

"I'm serious, it's my dad. He's not okay," she said, and watched then as they rode right on by him. Jimmie was standing at the next stop, waving and pretending to be happy to see her. He swore angrily when they passed him too. And she made a face at her old boss, the sourpuss, when they came to him, and laughed.

The bus driver even laughed.

There was a man from her past at every corner, and there were women, some she recognized, and some she'd never met; strangers but for the way they looked at her. But they didn't matter anymore either. When the driver finally stopped the bus, Anne Marie was ready to get off, and thanked him.

"Where am I going?" she asked.

"Right there," he said, and motioned to a run-down shotgun house with a red lamp glimmering on the porch. "Don't let the light fool you. You'll be safe inside. And you'll be welcome."

CHAPTER FIFTY-TWO

Anne Marie had never been in a women's shelter before. "I'm sorry, I probably don't belong here," she said, turning to leave.

"Why not?" a very large matron, hands on her hips and looking every bit a voodoo queen, asked. "You got somewhere else to go?"

Anne Marie shook her head. "No, but.... Really, I'm sorry if I woke you."

"That's right, you did," the woman said. "So you'd better get your sorry ass in here, cause I don't like gettin' woke for nothin', ya hear. Now come on."

Anne Marie smiled and entered another world.

"First thing we gotta do, is get you out of them wet clothes. What'd you do, go swimmin' in the fountain?"

Anne Marie followed her down a long hall, cactus in tow, past three rooms of women and children in various stages of sleep. One little girl was whimpering, one woman half waved, and one woman lay trembling.

"No drinkin' or drugs allowed," the voodoo queen said. "But I got a soft spot for that one. I lace her coffee or she'd never get through the day."

Anne Marie nodded, trailing along. When they got to the laundry room, which was just beyond the kitchen, the woman had her strip, gave her a robe, and started her laundry. "What about your bag?"

Anne Marie hesitated. "It's a...." She opened her backpack and showed her. "A prom dress. I should wash it by hand." She'd rinsed it thoroughly with the hose, but it still had evidence of footprints all over it.

"Suit yourself." The woman motioned to the laundry tubs. "There's a line out back to dry. The bathroom's that way. Wait till the washer fills before you run a bath. There's Band-Aids and antiseptic in there too for your head," she said, assessing the wound with a sleepy but expert glance. "You want some coffee?"

"Yes, please," Anne Marie said.

"All right, I'll put some on. There's a couch in the front room you can have. I'll put you out a blanket and pillow. We get up around eight."

"Thank you," Anne Marie said, and wanted to hug her, voodoo queen and all, but she disappeared. It felt odd being alone in a strange house, with strange people, a stranger herself. Anne Marie hand-washed the dress as quietly as she could, and tiptoed outside to hang it on the line. Though it was nearing dawn, the moon shone bright.

The thought occurred to her, that she could be anywhere, and the moon would always be the same, always be there. Even when she couldn't see it, as her grandmother had said, it was there. And she was right. A feeling of well-being accompanied her inside. She helped herself to a cup of coffee and sat down at the table, listening for when the washer stopped. The coffee was an eye opener. She added more powdered creamer, and tried it again. Much better. Another cup and her clothes were ready for the dryer. She took a bath then, and came out and put on warm underwear, jeans and shirt, checked outside to see that the dress was still there, and dragged the cactus back down the hall to the front room.

The couch was well-worn and practically embraced her as she burrowed down and covered up, for what was to be a brief but restful sleep.

"Lady? Lady, are you awake?"

Anne Marie thought she heard a child's voice, maybe Laura's, and opened her eyes to a tiny, cherub-like face just inches from hers.

"Lady?"

Anne Marie smiled. It was a little boy. "Breakfasts," he said, and took off running.

Anne Marie folded the blanket, made a stop in the bathroom, and joined the others in the kitchen. "Good mornin'," the voodoo queen said. "You got toast."

Anne Marie turned, stared a second, and caught on. She was to make toast for the whole crew. Everyone had a job to do, even the little guy. He was setting out silverware.

The voodoo queen handed Anne Marie a muddy-colored cup of steaming-hot coffee. "I'm Rosalee," she said, searching Anne Marie's eyes for something, and then nodding her approval. "Here's the rules. No one asks any questions just to be nosey, and no one has to say anything they don't want."

Anne Marie smiled. That suited her just fine. "Thank you," she said, and the bustle of preparing breakfast for twelve continued. Bacon and eggs, toast and grits, orange slices, coffee, and whole milk.

"All surplus," Rosalee said, "from here and there, so no one's beholden." They sat down to eat, some at the table, some at the counter, and one on a foot stool, which had her practically sitting on the floor. Anne Marie chose to stand, not wanting to take anyone's place. The children were served before the rest.

Anne Marie's first mouthful didn't set very well; she'd gone too long without eating. "Just sip your coffee a minute," Rosalee said. "And you'll be fine."

Anne Marie did as she was told, and was soon enjoying the meal along with everyone else. One of the women had a job interview scheduled, another was going to meet up with her and watch her children while she went to the unemployment office. One had a doctor's appointment. And another was going to court for the third time. They all turned to Anne Marie. She hesitated.

"I bought an old prom dress," she said. "And when I put it on, I felt pregnant. I believe the dress came from New Orleans, and I'm trying to find out what happened to the baby. I think her name was Laura."

Rosalee looked at her along with everyone else. "And how do you know all this?" She held her hand up, letting Anne Marie know again, that she didn't have to answer. It was up to her. No hard feelings, no pressure.

"I hear voices," Anne Marie said. Every woman in the room nodded. "And I see auras. I see dead people. And I don't know how to let go."

"Amen," Rosalee said. "Who's turn is it to wash?"

"Mine." Anne Marie welcomed something to do, to say thank you, to do her part, and worked at a feverish pace. Angela's Fashions would be opening soon, and the more she thought about it, the more apprehensive she was becoming. If she didn't go now, she never would.

CHAPTER FIFTY-THREE

Anne Marie phoned her mother and let her rant and rave for about a minute before interrupting. "Mom, I need a favor."

"What?" Silence.

"I need to ship you part of the cactus overnight, but it's more money than I have, and...."

"You mean you don't have any money?"

"No, I have money," she lied. Six dollars in addition to the vintage shop owner's ten could hardly be called money under the circumstances. "Listen, I don't have much time." Three minutes was all she'd paid for. "When you get the cactus, you have to pot it right away. I'm sending it collect."

"You're sending what collect?"

"The top half of the cactus. It broke off."

"You took your cactus with you?"

"Yes, I had to. Now please, listen."

"I am listening, stop saying that."

"All right, but it's important."

"When are you coming home?"

"Tomorrow, late. Plant the cactus right away. Milt said to let it dry out twenty-four hours or so, so when I get home it'll be too late. Okay?"

"Okay. By the way, Judy got engaged. Phil bought her a ring."

Anne Marie smiled. "Tell her I'll come see her when I get back."

"And I got more tea. Miss Colorado says you're supposed to call her. She says it's very important and that you left without telling her, too."

"Mom, I've gotta go. I'm running out of time. I'll see you Wednesday. And thanks, okay?"

"Okay."

"Wait! How are you doing?"

"Fine. I feel good. Don't forget to call your neighbor," her mother said, and the line went dead.

Anne Marie decided to wait until later to phone Miss Colorado, since she needed more change anyway. She walked the sixteen blocks from the parcel service to Magazine Street, dragging the cactus behind her, and had to stop to try and catch her breath and focus. Everything was a blur. It's nerves, she told herself, when the thought that she could possibly have suffered a concussion last night crossed her mind. It's just nerves. You're fine. You've never been stronger in your life. You could run a mile. Two miles. Three.

She stepped out into traffic and heard screeching tires, then a horn, and backed out of the way. "Sorry," she told the man, when he yelled at her for scaring him to death.

"Pay attention!"

"I am, now," she said, and crossed when the light changed. Angela's Fashions was but a means to an end, a way to put this all behind her and get on with her life. Think of it that way, she kept saying in her mind. Think of it that way. She opened the wrought iron gate, pulled the cactus through, and climbed the stairs. She didn't dare glance at the corner window. Just go inside. She entered the vestibule and hesitated.

"Are you here for your fitting?" she heard someone ask, and turned. But no one was there. She knocked on the door.

"Come in."

Anne Marie found herself on the other side.

"Can I help you?"

"Yes. Are you Angela?"

The woman shook her head and smiled tentatively. "I'm her daughter. What can I do for you?"

"Uh...." Anne Marie drew a deep breath. "I'm not sure." How could she explain? This was unreal, and yet so very real. Nothing had changed. The room was exactly as she remembered it. "I have this dress that I bought, I mean that someone bought a long time ago, and...."

The woman took on a somewhat wary stance.

"I'm sorry," Anne Marie said, noticing and wondering why. "I just have a few questions and then I'll leave."

The woman nodded, watched as Anne Marie removed the prom dress from her backpack, and stepped closer. "Oh my," she said, reaching for it. "I used to have one just one like this."

Anne Marie's heart skipped a beat. "Are you Laura?"

"No, mercy, where are my manners? My name is Jeanine. Where did you get this anyway?"

"From a vintage shop in Ohio."

"Ohio, really? That far? I wonder whatever happened to mine?"

Anne Marie shook her head. "Was the dress made here?"

"I don't know, it looks like it could have been. Mom made each one a little different. It's amazing how we wanted them all alike back then. I was a junior in high school."

Anne Marie stared. Surely this meant she hadn't come all this way for nothing. There was a connection. "Could I speak to your mother?"

"My mother?" The woman glanced over her shoulder. "No, I'm sorry, you can't. She doesn't see customers anymore."

Anne Marie hesitated. "I won't take much of her time. I just want to ask her if...."

The woman stopped her. "Mother has Alzheimers," she said. "Well not quite, but something similar. She won't be able to help you. What do you want to know anyway?" She handed the dress back.

"I want to know who she made this for, who it belonged to."

The woman shook her head and apologized again, but with irony in her voice. "You don't understand. She doesn't even know who *she* is anymore, let alone...."

Tears welled up in Anne Marie's eyes, silent tears that ultimately slid down her face and onto the dress as she stood to leave. "Thank you. I just.... It's just that I've come so far."

"Look," the woman said, feeling bad. "If it'll help, I'll show it to her. Sometimes...." She drew a breath and sighed. "Sometimes she remembers things. Who knows? Come on." She took Anne Marie by the hand. "Leave the cactus here. The stairs are steep."

And narrow. First up a flight and over, and then down.

"When mother first opened the shop, the sub-floor was all she could afford. She likes it down here, now that it doesn't flood anymore. She lives here. She won't even go to the doctor anymore. He comes to her. He calls it the dungeon."

A dungeon it was not. It was home, it was warm and cozy, sanctuary to a frail little woman of ninety-nine who, though ancient indeed, was not at all frightening in this light.

Anne Marie sat breathless, glancing anxiously from one to the other as the woman's daughter tried getting her attention.

"Mother?"

The old woman was bent over her work, sewing stitches back and forth on a tiny swatch of useless fabric.

"Mother? Angela?" The daughter shrugged. "Sometimes it works," she said, with the utmost respect. "Mother?"

Anne Marie didn't see any hope in this. The old woman never even looked up.

"Are you ready for lunch?"

"No."

The daughter smiled. "She won't eat till noon, right on the dot. She knows time, but...."

Anne Marie gave her the dress, and the daughter nodded. It was worth a try. "Mother, did you make this dress? Is it one of yours?"

The woman kept sewing.

"It would have been back around the time of my junior prom. Do you want to take a look?"

"No."

"Are you sure?" the daughter leaned down to see into her eyes. "This girl has come a long way. Mother?"

"No."

The daughter stood up and looked at Anne Marie. "I'm sorry."

Anne Marie nodded. So was she.

"Go away," the old woman said. "Leave me alone."

"Mother...?"

"I said go away." She raised her head and looked at Anne Marie. "Go away."

Her daughter apologized for her again and again upstairs. "She's never like that. I don't know what came over her."

"It's all right," Anne Marie said. "I shouldn't have bothered her or you." She turned the cactus around, and was folding the dress to put back into her backpack, when suddenly there was a noise behind them.

It was Angela. "Yes, may I help you?" the old woman asked, steadying herself in the doorway with her cane.

Her daughter's mouth dropped. "Oh my God," she uttered.

Anne Marie stared. Angela was no older than fifty in her eyes, and in a hurry. "Come on, come on," she said, with a wave of her hand. "Let's fit your dress, and see what we can do. Come on, come on."

Her daughter stepped back out of the way, in awe. She hadn't seen her mother like this in years.

Anne Marie didn't know what to do.

"The dressing room is right through there. Do you need help?"

Anne Marie shook her head at first, but then nodded. "I can't believe this," Jeanine whispered, following her and trembling so much she couldn't fasten a single button. "This is the way she used to be. This is my mother. I can't believe it."

"It's the dress," Anne Marie said, and smiled. If nothing else, if this was all she came for, one last fitting for this old woman, then she could live with that. It was a reason. Maybe there was no Laura. Maybe this was why she was here.

"Aren't you ready?" Angela asked impatiently.

Jeanine peeked out from behind the curtain, then back at Anne Marie, and smiled a little girl's smile. Her mother had pins in her mouth and tape measure in hand. "Thank you," she told Anne Marie. "Thank you."

CHAPTER FIFTY-FOUR

Anne Marie's fear that Angela would notice the alterations to the prom dress, let alone the repairs and condition, proved unwarranted. Angela seemed quite pleased with the fit and satisfied with her work. Understandably though, she tired within minutes. Jeanine encouraged Anne Marie to stay as she helped her mother back to her room.

While she was gone, Anne Marie changed back into her regular clothes, and sat looking around, hoping something might jog her memory, Laura's memory.

"I talked her into a short nap," Jeanine said, returning. "Will you join me for coffee? I know I sure could use a cup."

Anne Marie glanced at the clock on the wall. "Yes, thank you."

Jeanine hung the closed sign in the door for the first time during business hours in Angela's Fashions' history. She wanted to know the whole story behind the dress, and didn't want to chance being interrupted.

"Oh my, that is so sad," she said, mulling it all over. "And you have no idea who this Laura might be?"

Anne Marie shook her head.

"I wish there was something I could do."

Anne Marie smiled. "There is. Tell me where I can buy the best pralines in New Orleans."

Jeanine laughed. "Now that I know." She told Anne Marie how to get to Aunt Sally's, and hugged her before she left.

It was a gorgeous day, the sun shining bright, and warm and breezy. The cactus cart was still a drag, but amazingly for some reason, the plant itself looked good. It no longer seeped where the top had broken off, and it appeared to be coming back to life.

Anne Marie felt good as well. She walked up to Canal Street and over to Decatur and bought a box of pralines for $7.50 plus tax, couldn't resist and bought one for herself, and then she roamed the French Quarter. She had no memory of the place, so everything was new, the buildings, the balconies, the crowds, the market. She watched a juggler and a mime at length, the mime was very good, and found herself observing a painter in the midst of a watercolor.

"You need more blue," she told him, and he smiled.

"Go to the head of the class," he said. "I'm color blind."

Anne Marie laughed and looked closer. "In that case then, you need more red."

"Sit down," he urged, changing his canvas and wanting to paint her. "Right here." He patted the seat next to him.

"Sorry, maybe next time," she said. The mime converged on them with a big frown on his face and imaginary tears.

"Don't go," he mimed, with his hands over his heart. "Stay."

Anne Marie smiled and dug into her pocket. She was down to her last four dollars. She showed him, and gave him one, which he folded and folded and pretended to put into his mouth. And just then she heard someone call her name.

"Anne Marie! Oh, thank God!"

It was Angela's daughter, Jeanine. Jeanine...?

"I've been looking for you everywhere! I've been to the bus station three times!"

Anne Marie smiled curiously. "Why?"

"Come on!" Jeanine grabbed her by the arm. "We have to hurry." She had her mini-van double parked at the corner. "I found Laura!"

"What?!" Anne Marie picked up her pace, the cactus rumbling along behind her. "Where?"

Jeanine explained in the van, panting and out of breath. "I called a friend of mine after you left. She went to the same prom as me. She said she remembered someone in a pink dress like mine being there, but couldn't remember who, so we started calling people. It turns out the girl was pregnant, like you said."

"You mean Laura?"

"No." Jeanine shook her head and swerved into the other lane. "Her mother. Helen Randolph."

Anne Marie stared. The name meant nothing.

"Darla said everybody at their table was talking about it at the prom, and that all the guys wanted to dance with her, and that her boyfriend got mad and they went outside, and that someone ripped her dress, and...."

Anne Marie shook her head in amazement.

"We'll have to hurry."

"To where?" Anne Marie asked, glancing at the cactus when they sped around the corner, to make sure it was still standing.

"To her house. It's in Metarie."

"How do you know?"

Jeanine glanced at her. "Sue called back after calling Elaine, and she remembered the guy's name, because Linda went out with him once when she was fifteen."

"Linda Martin?"

"Yes." Jeanine looked at her. "How did you know?"

Anne Marie shrugged. She wasn't sure.

Jeanine signaled and took a left. "So evidently, they married. This Helen Randolph and Dave Danzik. No one answered the phone, but we thought it was worth a chance. Darla's meeting us there. She knew Helen a little, they used to be friends when they went to Live Oak and she thought...."

Anne Marie smiled. When they pulled up in front of this Helen Danzik's house, there were cars parked everywhere. Not only was Jeanine's friend Darla waiting for them, pacing anxiously in the driveway, three other women were waiting along with her.

"No one's home," Darla declared. "What time's your bus leave?"

"Five-fifteen," Anne Marie said.

"Can you stay over?"

Anne Marie shook her head. With three dollars to her name, not hardly.

"Try a neighbor," Brenda suggested, the most fidgety of the group. "Sue, you go ask, you're good at that."

Sue rolled her eyes and went next door.

"We can't let you leave without knowing," Charlotte said. "For your sake as well as ours. Think," she told the rest, wanting ideas. And they all turned after a moment, watching Sue as she walked back down the drive.

"Well...?"

Sue shook her head and glanced away with tears welling up in her eyes. "Helen Danzik is dead. I can't believe this, I'm crying over someone I haven't seen in thirty years. I hardly knew her, for Christ sake."

"When?" Charlotte asked, the question on all their minds. "When did she die?"

"I don't know. Friday, Saturday. Her funeral's today. We show up, and her funeral's today."

"Where?" Darla asked.

"Oh no...." Brenda said, backing up. "Forget it."

"We can't. Besides, the woman didn't tell me where."

"Wait!" Charlotte ran to her car. "Maybe it's in the newspaper." She hurried back, turned to the obituary section, and found the listing with everyone looking over her shoulder. Helen Danzik indeed died on Friday, forty-nine years of age, and was being buried today at Metarie Cemetery.

"Let's go," Darla said, and for once in their lives they were all in agreement.

"Does anyone know how to get there?"

"Yes," Sue said. "Follow me."

Anne Marie didn't know what to think as she got back into Jeanine's van. These women were on a mission, and all old enough to be her mother. If they thought it was all right to crash a funeral, who was she to say otherwise?

"Don't worry," Jeanine said. "We'll get you to the bus on time."

Anne Marie nodded, the very least of her worries at this moment. What if their being there caused more pain? What if the past is more harmful than good? What if...?

"Anne Marie?"

She turned to look at Jeanine and thought of her own mother.

"Are you okay?"

Anne Marie nodded. "I'm fine."

The cemetery was but a five-minute drive away. Sue slowed down as their procession neared the first funeral in progress, glanced in her mirror, and drove on when Charlotte waved her ahead. Wrong party. It was the next one, which besides the hearse had only two cars. The women pulled in one after another behind them and parked and got out, the sound of their car doors echoing off the tombs.

"Family and friends...."

Anne Marie swallowed hard.

"We are gathered here today on this somber occasion...."

A young woman dressed in black looked up when they approached and smiled bravely with tears in her eyes. This was her mother they were burying. This young woman was Laura.

CHAPTER FIFTY-FIVE

The minister was a tall, gaunt man who insisted everyone drop a clump of dirt on the casket in passing. "Ashes to ashes. Dust to dust."

"Amen."

"Let's wait for her over here," Darla said, brushing off her hands and pointing to a bench when the minister drew Laura aside to talk to her.

"Your mother would not want you to mourn," Anne Marie heard him say, speaking directly into her face. "Do you understand?"

Laura nodded, and glanced away.

"Laura?" He waited for her to look at him again. "I'm sorry," he said. "She was a good woman. Her pain is gone now."

"I wonder what she looked like," Charlotte asked. "She used to be pretty."

"I think her daughter looks a little like her," Darla said.

Brenda nodded, reaching for her cigarettes, and promptly put them away when each one of her friends frowned at her. "What? Do you think she smoked?"

Darla sighed. "I feel like a hypocrite. Where were we all these years?"

"I don't know. Getting married, having kids."

"Getting divorced."

"Getting married again."

"Having a hysterectomy."

Sue heaved a heavy sigh. "We should've been here for her."

Laura shook the minister's hand and walked toward them, a very graceful young woman with proud posture. "Thank you for coming," she said, with the slightest hint of an accent.

"We knew your mother long ago," Brenda said. "Some of us went to school with her."

"I knew her in junior high."

"So did I."

Laura smiled, looking thoughtfully from one to the next, and Anne Marie noticed something, first in her aura, then in the very careful way she watched the mouths of those who spoke. Laura was deaf. She couldn't hear a word they were saying. Nor had she heard her mother's voice.

"What did she die from?" Sue asked, suddenly overwhelmed with grief.

Laura hesitated. "Breast cancer."

All the women reacted with the same expression, dread and fear.

"Listen...." Jeanine said, with a heavy pause and having to clear her throat. "Could we talk to you a minute?"

Laura nodded, motioned to the man waiting for her, and the women all sat down around one another.

Jeanine drew a deep breath. "Something happened to us today that made us remember who we were, who we are. And we wanted to help, to do something. We all have children. We all have daughters. We are daughters." She looked at Anne Marie. "This young girl showed up on my doorstep today, and because of her I saw my mother differently." Tears filled her eyes. "I'm sorry," she said, and Brenda put her arm around her. "It's because of your mother as well."

They all nodded, wanting Laura to understand.

"I knew her best," Darla said. "You look so much like her. Oh, the stories I could tell."

Laura smiled, reading every word she said.

"Did she have a good life?" Sue asked, her voice cracking. "I'd like to think she had a good life."

"She did," Laura said. "Not a perfect one, but a good one."

"And your dad? How is he?"

Laura glanced at the distinguished man standing solemnly at the foot of his wife's grave, a glance that revealed volumes to Anne Marie. He was a good man, protective and loving, a good husband, a good father. "He'll be fine, I think," Laura said, squaring her shoulders as if in support of him, what he'd been through, what he faced.

Charlotte blew her nose and dabbed at her eyes. "Anne Marie, tell her about the dress."

Laura looked at her. "What dress?"

Anne Marie hesitated, her bottom lip quivering. "About a month ago...."

Laura stiffened. About a month ago, was when her mother had slipped into a coma.

"I bought this dress." Anne Marie clutched her backpack with both hands. "It's a prom dress. And when I put it on...."

Laura started to cry. "Oh my God."

Anne Marie didn't know what to do. She took the dress out.

"Oh my God. Oh my God," Laura kept saying.

"When I put it on, I felt pregnant."

"You were," Laura said. "She was, that was me." She reached for the dress and cradled it gently to her heart. "That was me. Oh my God!"

The women sat rocking one another and crying.

"She gave up so much for me. Practically everything. Her family.... Look around, they didn't even come today. And all because of me."

"No," Anne Marie said, thinking of her own mother. "She lived for you. I kept hearing her voice. I kept hearing it over and over." She turned Laura's face to hers. "I don't hear it anymore. You have to listen now."

Laura shook her head. "I can't. I can't hear it."

"Yes, you can. Open your eyes and listen," Anne Marie said instinctively. "Open your eyes. Look at her dress, look at yourself. Look everywhere. Because she's there. She wants you to know that she will never leave you, ever. She's your mother. She will always be there. Always."

"Even when you don't want them to be," Darla said, and wiped her eyes. Everyone hugged and laughed. They'd cried enough.

"Let me tell you about the time your mother and I climbed into the window of the principal's office. Your mother had the flashlight and I had the watermelon. He'd given us demerits that day for being late from lunch, and...."

It was time for Anne Marie to leave. "No, don't," she told Jeanine when she rose to leave also. "I'll take the bus. Please." She got the cactus out of the van, and from the gate, looked back at the circle of women gathered in the cemetery, laughing and crying, telling their stories, glowing. And way off in the distance, walking among the tombs and reading the names, was her grandmother, who turned then and smiled.

CHAPTER FIFTY-SIX

Were it not for Rosalee, Anne Marie's torn bus ticket could have been a problem. "Don't tell 'em it was stolen or vandalized," she'd said, painstakingly taping it all back together. "Lord, they'll make a big to-do and you'll never get to leave. If it's a man, say your little boy did it. If it's a woman, blame your little girl."

It was a man, and it worked. In fifteen minutes, Anne Marie would be on her way home. She changed her last two dollars into coins at the counter and phoned Miss Colorado. "I'm sorry I didn't come see you before I left. I just...."

"That's all right, dear. How are you?"

"Okay. I'll be home tomorrow. I only have a few minutes. My mom said you needed to talk to me about something important."

"I do. Well, I did. It's about your rent."

"I paid it."

"When?"

"Last week. I gave it to the Super."

"The Super? Oh my. Well, don't worry about it then. I'll talk to John."

"Why? Where's the Super?"

"Who knows. They'll find him though. He never goes far. He just forgets where he lives sometimes."

Anne Marie shook her head.

"Oh, and the girls upstairs asked about you. They were worried they hadn't seen. Your mother told them you were fine."

"My mother?"

"Yes, she was here at the time, and we all had tea."

Anne Marie pictured them all together and smiled. What a bunch. "I'm sorry I wasn't there."

"Us too. Did you find Laura?"

"Yes. I'll tell you all about it when I get home. Which reminds me, what did you want to say before I left?"

"Hmmm, let me think." When Miss Colorado hesitated, Anne Marie feared she would run out of time. "I remember now. I wanted to tell you about a safe place you could stay."

"Oh. Well thank you. I found one."

"I know. How is Rosalee?"

Anne Marie stared. "She's fine. Did you send me there?"

"No, dear. I followed you. That was exhausting enough. I've done nothing but sleep since."

Anne Marie smiled. "So. Did anyone else come calling?"

"No, not that I know of."

Good, Anne Marie thought, they're all gone.

"But about Danny...."

Anne Marie stared ahead. "What about him?"

"I don't know. I guess I'm just not sure he's the one anymore."

"Why? What do you mean?"

"I don't know," Miss Colorado said, and that's where the conversation ended. When the operator asked for an additional ninety-five cents to be deposited, Anne Marie had but a dime left of her own.

Exhausted herself and hungry, she boarded the bus, and sat down and sighed as she tucked the cactus in next to her. She really should have told Danny when she was leaving, she knew that now, and didn't even have the magic of the dress to draw him back. Maybe it was never meant to be.

She dozed off and on, but didn't really sleep until after they'd changed buses in Memphis, and from there she slept until mid-day. Her stomach growled. For breakfast it was water, and now for lunch, water again.

The more water she drank, the less hungry she felt. She leaned her head back and gazed out the window. This part of the country, hidden in darkness on her way down, was scenic and colorful now, but almost hypnotic, and after a while she could hardly keep her eyes open.

She saw Ellie's crows along the side of the road. They all turned their curious little heads and watched her go by. Then it started to rain, a downpour, and all she saw was rushing water. She drifted

217

more and more, lulled by the sound, and when she woke, found herself looking at the woman next to her. The seat had originally been empty.

"Hello."

Anne Marie smiled.

"If you want to know where I came from, I can't tell you. I only know where I'm going."

"Oh," Anne Marie said, yawning. "And where would that be?"

"North. All the way, as far as I can go."

Anne Marie glanced out the window, and with the absence of the sun, could only hope they were headed in the right direction.

"Would you like a sandwich? I have two."

Food, Anne Marie thought. Food. "No, thank you. I...."

"Come on. Here," the woman said, handing her one. "I hate eating alone. Come on, eat."

Anne Marie nodded and took a bite. The bread was sliced thick and warm, with what tasted like cream cheese inside, only sweeter, that melted heavenly in her mouth.

"I just made them."

Anne Marie devoured both halves.

"Tea?" The woman took out a thermos and just happened to have two cups.

Anne Marie recognized the brew. "Thank you. This is delicious," she said, taking one sip and then another. "It's been a while since I...."

"I know," the woman said, patting her gently on the knee. "I know. Now if you'll excuse me, this is where I get off."

Anne Marie smiled, and watched her walk to the front and disappear. If the woman were in her imagination, it didn't matter. Anne Marie was no longer hungry.

CHAPTER FIFTY-SEVEN

Anne Marie opened her eyes and stared. The bus was at her home station and most everyone had already gotten off. "Wow!" She hurried to the door, dragging the cactus behind her, and got off with the last straggling few. The rain had stopped and the sun was out, for which she was grateful, since she'd be walking.

She turned the cactus around, the wheels barely functioning now, and smiled in surprise when she raised her eyes and glanced ahead.

"Well, it's about time," Danny said, with that grin of his, and she ran into his arms. There was so much to say; to explain, to ask, but it would all have to wait. He kissed her again and again. "God, I've missed you!"

She held on tight.

"I wasn't sure which bus you'd be on. I've been here twice today," he said, and noticed the cut on the side of her face. "Wait a minute, what's this?"

Anne Marie shrugged. It would be nice to be able to lie, to avoid telling the truth, for his sake if nothing else, but she couldn't. "I got mugged."

"What? See, didn't I tell you?"

Anne Marie smiled, reassuring him when he searched her eyes. "I'm fine. It was just a bump on the head, that's all."

"And Laura?" He didn't like her going, but deep down understood. "Did you find her?"

Anne Marie nodded.

"Come on." He took her by the hand and reached for the cactus cart, anxious to leave, to get on with the rest of their lives, but stopped abruptly. "What the hell?"

Anne Marie laughed. At first she thought his reaction was to the top of the plant being gone, but it was the wheels not rolling that had gotten his attention. He examined them close. Both axles were off track, and took nothing to pop back into place. Only then did he notice the cactus.

"What happened?"

Anne Marie told him all about it in the Camaro as they drove across town, the T-tops out, and the wind in her hair. She told him everything. And all he did in the end was shake his head and smile.

"So you left the dress?"

Anne Marie nodded, and with that, so did he. "Then it's just you and me now, huh?"

She smiled.

They stopped by her mother's, who was so happy to see them together, she actually hugged both Danny and Anne Marie. The cactus had arrived early this morning, was planted, and sat in the kitchen window.

"It might be too moist in here for it," Anne Marie said.

Her mother laughed. "You take care of yours, and I'll take care of mine."

"Deal," Anne Marie said, and promised to come back tomorrow for lunch.

Her mother told her about the film then. "Vince said it was ruined. There wasn't a picture on it. I'm sorry," she said.

Anne Marie nodded. So was she. But then again, maybe it was just as well. They probably would have been too painful to view. "Mom...." Anne Marie hesitated at the door.

Rebecca looked at her.

"Dad wasn't a very nice man, was he?"

Her mother shook her head, her eyes clouding instantly with memories. "No. But there was a time...." She shrugged, enough said.

Anne Marie smiled. "I'll see you tomorrow." She and Danny stopped by the vintage shop owner's next, and dropped off the Pralines and the woman's change.

"Good news," Rita reported, already into the box and licking her fingers. "We're allowed back in the store Monday. Boy, are we going to be busy!"

Anne Marie said she was looking forward to it, and as she glanced around at the maze of new boxes, smiled. The radio was playing Rita's favorite oldies station, and much to Anne Marie's delight, she didn't know a single word to the song.

They stopped by Judy and Phil's flat then. Phil was working, but Judy was home and waiting. "He asked me! Can you believe it?" she said, showing off her ring. "It was just like Miss Colorado said. Isn't it beautiful?"

Anne Marie nodded. It was, most definitely. "And you say Phil picked this out all by himself?"

Judy laughed.

The veteran was sitting on the stoop when they finally got to the apartment, and toasted her arrival home with a round of ice cold beer. It went to Anne Marie's head.

"Come on," Danny said, helping her to her feet. "It's been a long day."

"Not really. I slept all the way."

Miss Colorado heard them out in the hall.

"Oh, Anne Marie, dear. You're home."

"That's right, I am," Anne Marie said, hugging the tiny little woman. "I am home, aren't I?"

Miss Colorado smiled. "Yes, dear," she said, meaning they found the Super. "You're home."

Anne Marie introduced her to Danny. "He's the telephone man."

"I know, dear. So nice to see you," she said to Danny.

Danny smiled.

"He's the one," Anne Marie whispered close. "He is."

"Oh? Are you sure?"

Anne Marie looked up at Danny. "Yes."

"Then wait right here," Miss Colorado said, and returned with a petal box.

"What's this for?"

"You'll know," Miss Colorado said.

Anne Marie took it with her into her apartment, but wouldn't touch it again until she and Danny bathed and were washed clean.

"What is it, Anne Marie?" he asked, in the bedroom when she finally opened it and looked up at him.

"It's me, Danny. It's who I am?"

There was lavender, her grandmother, jasmine, her mother, cinnamon, the earth, lemon, the sun, sage, the wind.... "It's me."

Danny's heart quickened, his breath drawn deep as she dusted the contents all around her in bed and reached for his hand.

"What do I give to you, Anne Marie?"

"What do you have?"

He brought a handful of flower petals to his mouth and brushed them back and forth across his lips. "My heart and my soul," he said. And she welcomed him, mind, body, and spirit.

Sometime in the night, the cactus flowered. Sometime in the night, Anne Marie and Danny slept.

From the author

I would like to express my gratitude to the Erie Shore and Northeast Ohio Writers for always being there. And to thank editors Ellie King, Beth Vanderpool, Linda Durnbaugh, Janice Fazio, Catherine March, and Jack Friedberg for their endless hours of pouring over the manuscript, for their keen eyes, and for their kindred hearts. And to John Myers, as always, for paving the way.

Thank you....